Ancestries

Yabome Gilpin-Jackson

ISBN: 9781089218029

DEDICATION

To all who will find themselves in these pages because all the experiences in these stories are real, although none of the characters are.

&

To my Ancestors…

To my parents, Haja Fatmatta Kanu & Dr Sheka Hassan Kanu;

To my Maternal Grandparents, Haja Yabome Sesay & Sorie Ibrahim Bangurah;

To my Paternal Grandparents, Haja Fatmatta (Tity) Kamara & Hassan Kanu;

& To those that were before them…

I owe my legacy of life & dedicate this odyssey of rootedness & belonging to you.

If you nor sabi ouseye you comot, you nor go sabi ouseye you dey go.

Transliteration:
If you want to know where you are going, you have to know where you come from.

Sierra Leonean Proverb

CONTENTS

ACKNOWLEDGMENTS

I owe the inspiration for this short story collection to all who read its prequel *Identities: A short story collection* and reached out to me to share the impact it had on them. I heard from people of all races and backgrounds in addition to the primary audience it was intended for —Global Africans, that community of peoples born on or off the continent who live a significant part of their lives in global spaces.

I heard from a Japanese colleague who sought me out specifically to tell me: "As a second-generation Nagasaki descendent, the first story in your book, *Identities*, gave me immediate insight into why I feel anxiety whenever I'm in America and someone asks—where are you from? or where in Japan are you from? I realised I get anxious because the story of Nagasaki almost always then overshadows the story of me." White friends and colleagues reached out to say that reading Identities gave them new insights into awkward interactions they have had that they did not understand. One wrote that my writing on identity and the question where are you from, "helps me understand why I feel squirmy and wiggly in some of these cases, and not so in others."

Africans I met at book signings or readings who have felt separated from their African identity shed tears. Global Africans on and off the continent told me: "This was so real for me!" "The stories resonated so much!" "Please keep writing!" "This is every immigrant's story!" The best representation of this came from my Kenyan-Canadian friend and editor Evaline Njoki who wrote of Identities:

> *SOAR sis SOAR!! Loved reading your book, your words transported me to a world so familiar. Your book felt like HOME to me...love it. Love you.*

Thank you for your partnership and laser editorial eye, Njoki!

A special acknowledgment to my relative Syllona Kanu, of Sierra Leonean and Irish descent, who in sharing the impact of *Identities*, casually mentioned: "Then there's me and all the times I get asked:

What are you?" Thereafter, just like the 'spot the car' game, I started hearing about this experience of multiracial peoples everywhere—from one-on-one conversations to podcasts. That inspired the first story in this collection and the shards of it throughout the book. To each and every one of you, thank you for the love and inspiration to write on. We are on this journey together.

Thank you to my closest community of supporters, my family, especially my Yayo (mom) and my husband, Adelana Gilpin-Jackson. Deepest gratitude also to my family and friends who pre-read this collection and were my first reviewers. I love and cherish each of you. And to my children, Kayla, Jaaziah and Perez, you inspire me always to make safe spaces for you to grow, realise your identities and belong. A special acknowledgement to my son Jaaziah who was my accountability partner on this and a non-fiction book I was working on at the same time: "How far are you now Mummy?! How many more pages? Mummy, you should go work—when is your deadline again? We need to work on a schedule for you so you don't keep slacking off and sleeping!" You are the best Project Manager a mother can have. Thank you!

1. WHAT ARE YOU?

I pull up to the restaurant and park, turning off the ignition but leaving the engine on idle, a signal of my uncertainty. I sit, tan knuckles taut around the steering wheel at the ten and two o'clock positions. Sweat beads pop to my forehead to match the Vancouver rain falling on my car. I swear the sound of pelting rain connecting with the windshield wipers is mocking me. Every swish sounded the *lose* and every swoosh, *er.* I increase the wiper speed as the rain comes down harder. *Lose-er, lose-er, lose-er.*

What if this is a hoax and she's a no show?

Lose-er, lose-er, lose-er!

Fuck!! I hit the steering wheel with my right palm, then let my forehead rest in its centre for a moment.

I consider driving off. Then look up and catch sight of the flashing red ENTER sign. I'm curious about what lies behind it, so I inhale, hold the air in, then let it leak slowly out. I turn off the ignition and reach for the door. I swing my legs and my feet hit the ground. I am committed now. Besides, running away is no longer my style. The last time I ran away I was 15, pimply and in tenth grade. This kid Kevin had been staring at me whenever mom dropped me off but he never said anything to me. Until the morning of the day I ran away when he asked me at recess: "Hey Zoe! What are you?" I didn't even know he knew my name.

Hey Zoe! What are you? The tape plays in my mind now like it did then. I start walking towards the restaurant. I try to kick some leaves but they are too soaked to move so I kick at some stones instead, then flinch at the déjà vu. My feet are recreating the same movements they'd beat along the sidewalk path all the way home on that similar autumn day when I ran away.

I walk towards the side door of the restaurant. My strides slow and my feet stop beside the dumpster at the entrance. My hands reach into my raincoat pocket and pull out my Marlboros. I keep trying to quit this habit. Not today. I inhale deeply, eyes closed, head tilted against the dumpster. I enjoy the smoke coursing down my lungs. I hold the smoke for a few and exhale my nerves out into the rings of smoke now dancing in the rain above my head. My heart rate slows and I open my eyes, watching the leaves all around me. These ones belong to a tree that had turned shades of reddish yellow. I look for the different shapes and figures I like to spot from the patterns they've made on the ground. My mind tells me the leaves are beautiful.

Beautiful! You are beautiful.

That was my mom's response when I asked her what Kevin had asked me. I screamed at her:

What am I? What am I? Who's my fucking daddy!

I had stood staring at her. Shock mixed in with the volcanic rage I'd felt erupting from my chest. Just like I didn't know Kevin knew my name, I didn't know I could swear.

Mom had stared back at me. She took a swig of the sherry I'd found her drinking when I came home. She walked across the kitchen and slapped me square across the face, then turned, walked wobbly to her room and slammed the door. I remember thinking the neighbours attached to us by the shared wall of our town homes must have heard the door slam. I'd stood, suddenly aware I was winded. I started retching. Oxygen seemed to have drained from the air. I couldn't catch my breath and no sound came from my mouth when I tried to speak or scream. I ran to the sink and splashed water on my face till I could breathe. And in the moment after I could hear myself think again, my brain said: *you should run away.* So, I grabbed my bag and ran out the back door.

I hear a creaking sound and see the restaurant's side door swinging open. I drop the rest of my cigarette and quickly step over it, rubbing it into the ground with my boot toe. I have leftover shame from my runaway days. I don't like being caught in the act of smoking. I smile at the person coming through the door as I fish for mint in my purse. I find one, pop it in my mouth and move to catch the open door. Then I notice someone huddled on the other side of the dumpster, sheltering from the rain. I stop in my tracks and she darts away to avoid me but I follow her around the side.

I drop my hood to show my face. I smile to show I'm friendly, then stretch out my hands to offer her a Marlboro and the change in my pocket. Her face lights up at the sight of the offering but she hesitates. I nod towards my hand, signalling I want nothing in return. She lifts her head long enough to meet my eyes and offers me a wide smile of relief, from browned teeth with front ones missing. She mouths *thank you, thank you,* grabbing the lifelines from my hands before darting away again, still repeating *thank you.* I hear a yelp once she's out of sight. I marvel at the speed of her disappearing act as my brain acknowledges that could have been me. I wonder what she's running from. I used to go visit my runaway shelter close by once a month to get to know people, hear their stories and share a meal with the ones who were becoming friends. I stopped going when my friend Vanessa disappeared. It's been a few years, but I still look around when I drive by, hoping I'd spot her one of these days.

I'm in the restaurant and look around for my lunch date. The host stationed by the side door smiles and nods:

"You meeting someone? You look around or you go to the front and he show you by name in the book."

I smile back and choose to look around. It's Vancouver. Aminata will not be hard to spot. It's a typical Chinese restaurant like anywhere in the world. Red Chinese lanterns, a mix of round and square wooden tables and chairs, traditional antique wall art with Chinese features and symbols. This one had a few larger round tables with lazy suzys around the periphery of the room. I wonder if there is a Chinese restaurant superstore where you can order *The Chinese Restaurant in a Box*.

I realise I haven't seen a picture of Aminata because her WhatsApp profile image is a silhouette portrait of a woman in a headwrap made of Ankara fabric. I'm wondering why I hadn't thought to ask her for a photo or looked her up on social media when I think I spot her. She's tapping away on her iPhone, then looks up to scan the room just as I walk over. I stand behind the chair that I'm about to occupy. She half stands to greet me. We both say 'Hi' in synch. Nervous laughter. I'm holding too tightly to the back of the chair when I hear her say:

"Zoe, right? Will you sit?" There's a hint of amusement in her voice.

I oblige but can't stop staring. She keeps smiling, holding my eyes as we take each other in. My brain registers the thought: s*he's a darker-skinned, narrower framed version of who I see in the mirror every day.*

"Thanks for coming," she says. "How are you?"

The formality brings me back: "I'm good. And you?"

"I'm well. Very well, thank you. So, here we are—shall we order?" She says as she looks around and flags a server.

"I hear the food here is actually spicy. Thank God! What will you have?"

I pick the first semi-healthy combo of 4 items I could recognise—wonton soup, spicy fish with tofu, chow mein and spicy green beans. She chooses the hot and sour soup, Szechuan chicken hot pot, shrimp fried rice & some fusion combo of vegies with pork intestines that makes me cringe. I hear her tell the server we'll have combos 11 and 33 while I think of what to say. The server leaves.

"Why did you come looking for me?" I ask.

She pauses, then straight answers.

"Your father asked me to."

Another pause.

"Why did you agree to meet me?" she counters.

"Hmmm, I was curious, I guess. Always have been. About who my father is. Why didn't he come find me himself?"

My voice sounds pitchy. I pour green tea from the pot that had silently arrived and take a sip. I grimace because it is tepid.

"He did."

I take a big gulp of tea. I'm now grateful it's tepid.

"He came to do a lecture at University of British Columbia 10 years ago and attended a global alumnus gathering at the same time. He said he contacted your mom but she wouldn't let him see you. Said you were in a bad way and didn't need to be abandoned again. Told him she'll call the cops on him if he showed up."

I feel the dormant volcano in my belly begin to move. *10 years ago!*

I feel warm. She's taking me in.

"Daddy says he told your mom about the four of us and mom in the beginning, but she said it was ok for them to just have fun…until she became pregnant with you…"

The volcano moves up to my neck, so I stay silent, stonewalled.

"You should forgive her you know. Your mom. We all do crazy things when we are in love..." She trails off. I notice she is twirling her wedding band. I consider asking for her story. Decide not to. Instead I say: "Then why isn't he here now."

"He died last year. Cancer. He was with me in Ghana where I live for his medical treatments. He gave me your mom's details and your name and asked me to track you down when he knew he would pass on. I knew I had this work trip coming up to Montreal and Toronto and then Calgary and Vancouver so that's why I only reached out now."

The volcano moves back down below my heart, into my belly, then drops all the way to my feet. I suddenly feel drained, deflated, light-headed.

What are you? Fatherless!

"I'm sorry to hear that." I say to her. I'm a bit startled at how dispassionate I feel and sound.

The servers bring our food. I'm ravenous and dig right in.

"So…what was it like growing up? Why did your mom say you were in a bad way?"

I wipe a string of noodle from the side of my mouth.

"Well…look around here. That's what it was like. There was generally only one, maybe two other kids like me in my schools growing up. It was lonely. Too quiet. I had no other siblings at home. Mom worked hard and drank a bit too much in the evenings. Mom's parents never quite forgave her, you know…for being with a black man…Kids were civil at school but not really friendly outside that. In middle and high school there was usually also one or two kids from somewhere in the Caribbean or Africa. In high school, there was this Nigerian girl, Kemi. We got along for a while, but then mom got talking and laughing with her dad at a parent event at school. After that, Kemi wouldn't talk to me much and stopped inviting me over. In middle school, I had a fight with my mom because she wouldn't tell me about my dad. So, I ran away to the place they call the DTES around here."

"As in the Downtown Eastside! Up the road from here?"

"Yep! Only lasted two weeks. Came back badly bruised, almost raped and with a snorting habit. Spent lots of time in counselling, rehab and self-love programs through high school. I guess when it just happened is when…your dad…must have come."

"Oh!"

"I'm ok now though." I say it to reassure myself as much as her. "I'm grateful to be here and doing ok. I keep wondering what would have happened if it were now, y'know, with all the opioid stuff going around…"

"How about you?" I ask. "What was growing up like?"

"Well, mine was…busy in the way you wished for, I guess. My—our, other siblings and I are close. There's another girl Amal, she's 35. Two boys—Alim, short for Alimamy who's 33; and Abibu who just turned 30. All A names because our mom's name is Assiatu. I'm the oldest—just turned 37. I was always busy helping mom with them…Daddy was around but he was very busy. He travelled lots doing international agency contracts, you know…"

She sounds sympathetic. I notice I feel neither consoled nor empathetic to her plight of the travelling father. A least he came home.

I think she can sense my mood, because she stops talking and we both eat in silence for a while.

"Funny how my name starts with Z, huh," I say.

"Maybe," she says. "We have the same middle name though. I saw from the documents dad gave me that he named both of us Princess."

I feel a knot forming in my throat. I shake my head. A dead man I never knew shouldn't have so much power over me. I need a smoke. I need to leave.

"We look alike, you know. We both got his looks." She stated the obvious. I can't disagree.

"I can see that. And I love your cornrows."

"I love your big curly 'fro, girl! That's the look girls going for big natural hair work for and sometimes still have to use texturizer to get!"

We both burst out laughing. The tension starts evaporating from the air between us.

"You should come to Freetown. The others…including mom…they are open to meeting you. Alim and mom live there in the home we grew up in. Amal and Abibu will be home for the holidays and I'll go over there too. Plus, there are nieces and nephews. My son and daughter both look just like us too! There's so much I can show you. Even the exhibit about the Nova Scotia connections in Freetown…"

She's talking fast now. She can sense our time is almost up. She sounds excited and desperate. My head hurts. I feel like I'm about to crash from a high.

"I'll think about it."

Even I could hear how non-committal I sounded.

The server brings the bill. She grabs it. Shoots me a glare when I try to take it back.

"I'm African. I invited you to lunch and you are my younger sister. I am paying for our lunch." Her tone makes it clear there is no room to negotiate. I acquiesce.

She hands the server the bill with a credit card, then turns to face me fully.

"Please consider it. Since daddy told me I have been worried. I wasn't sure whether you'd agree to meet. Now that you have…we are blood…and we cannot be lost to each other forever. What if our children and grandchildren never know each other? Blood is thicker than water. We must stay connected."

'Yeah? But when blood is treated like a stain and doused to make it go away, it can run like water." I retort.

For a moment, she looks like she will start crying, but then she collects herself.

"May we at least take pictures?"

"Sure."

We pull out our phones. Capture selfies on both.

"I take picture for you too." The server is back with the receipt. We hand over our phones. He takes more pictures.

"I have to get back to work," I say.

She comes around. We hug. We stare at each other, arms around our shoulders. She pulls back, takes an A4 envelope that's stuffed too fat from her Gucci tote and hands it to me.

"It's a letter from your father. He also left you a gift, but says you must come to Sierra Leone to claim it. The paperwork for the gift from the lawyers is inside with his letter."

My hands are shaking and I drop the envelope on the table.

Her eyes are pleading: "please take it."

So I do. I pick it up and leave on jelly legs. I don't look back.

It's still raining out. I stand in the rain, lift my head and enjoy the feeling of water on my face, washing me, steadying me. The envelope feels like hot lead in my jacket pocket. I start walking, but this time I do not kick stones. I am crying and laughing out loud in the rain. *What am I, Kevin? I am free.*

I will never open the envelope. My grandson will, 65 years from this lunch date. By then, the gift will be worthless but the history priceless. He, not I, will make that trip to Sierra Leone. I will be too old and fragile to travel with him. He will trace relatives and find some of them, scattered all over the globe. He, not Aminata or I, will make our father's blood run thick again, reuniting us no matter our shade or hue. And I will lie on my deathbed, joyful that I gave my grandson the gift.

But today, I do not know any of that. I am just hysterically happy to be walking in the rain, free.

2. CHOPPED

"You should chop directly on the chopping board! You don't have to peel onto it as if you are peeling into a bowl!"

She paused and raised her head. He was wearing a look of disdain and reproach that matched his tone and it stung. She wiped the spontaneous moisture that sprung to her eyes, pretending she was tearing from the enzymes and oxides released from the onion spray. She opened her mouth to respond, but the words caught in her throat. Instead, her lips curled upwards, and she smiled. He glared back. He dropped his work bag, marched over, reached for the knife and pushed her over.

"Here! This *[chop]* is *[chop]* how *[chop]* to *[chop]* use *[chop]* a chopping board!"

His exasperated chopping demonstration might have worked if she was a child. Or stupid. But she was neither. She knew exactly how to use the chopping board. If he had asked, she would have explained that she preferred to peel onto the chopping board, because the muscle memories of her hand transported her home. That when she peeled onto the chopping board, she felt her Mama's presence. She would have said that that is the only time she remembers the words to the cooking song her Mama had made up to sing when she was in the kitchen with her daughters. Every other time she tried singing the song, she'd forget the arrangement of the words and ended up humming the tune instead.

Leh we cook for dem pikin dem. Tell God tenke for provision! For provision, for provision, tell God tenke for provision!

Let's cook for the children. Thank God for provision…

Me pikin dey learn for cook for im pikin dem, leh we show am how for cook. Leh we show am how for cook, how for cook, how for cook, leh we show am how for cook!

My child is learning how to cook for their children…

Me pikin go train im pikin for cook…leh e learn how e go train am. How e go train am, how e go train am, leh e learn how e go train am!

My child will teach their own child to cook…

She would have shared that she hoped to teach the daughter she'd dreamt of, that looked just like him, to sing that song too. But most importantly, she would have told him that peeling into the bowl was comfort. That was the one thing she most wanted and needed in this place.

He didn't ask. So instead of telling him all that, she let her voice remain strangled and her lips curl upwards into a sinister curve—something both forced and involuntary. He dropped the knife, shaking his head as he stomped away. If he wasn't so vexed, he might have caught the glassy deadness in her eyes.

~~~

He used to love looking into her eyes. Her eyes were their signal for their running rendezvous. They used to run together in the secret trails they had found in the forested areas behind the back gates of the home where their parents worked in Sussex, just off the peninsula of Freetown, Sierra Leone. They were both workers' children. He was the driver's son. She, the cook's daughter. When he walked to the house after school, he would intentionally walk through the kitchen to set up a study table at the back. He would greet her Mama
~~~

and talk to her in English. She would greet and talk back to him in Krenglish as we called it around here—an amalgam of Krio and English—and the same pidgin root from which Krio had sprouted. It was a ritual born of their house rules that all in the household were to speak primarily in English, even for people like Mama and I who were not English educated. We understood enough to get by. She might say to him:

"You de learn about overseas, 'bout 'Merica."

"No Mama Phebe, today I learnt about the British and the different Europeans who took over parts of Africa. But what I enjoyed most was learning about Canada Ma—that it was part of Britain and that some of our people were repatriates from there, Ma."

"I beg—dem big big book Englis' oh—na what be re-pat-ate!"

And while he answered her questions and explained the wonders of the world to her Mama, he would catch her eyes.

She would tell him with her eyes if it was a good day to go running in the trails or not. If it was a good day, she would come around the back after finishing her chores and signal to him. He'd leave the homework he was supposed to be doing and join her. They'd run with reckless abandon. He would pick up where he left off explaining to Mama and tell her more about his studies.

"One day, I will go to Canada to study. I will learn about that place and more about the world."

She would be mesmerised by the wonder of his dreams about this world—gazing through his eyes to the histories of Germany, Cuba, India, China, Australia and his favourite Canada. He showed her these places on maps and one of those days he said to her:

"Would you like me to teach you how to read?"

She hissed back at him— "For what? So I can stay telling Mama stories after you go and I be here cooking?!"

They fell laughing into each other's arms. He promised her then, while drinking in the centre of her eyes, that he wouldn't leave her there to cook for the rest of her life. For a moment, she believed him, but she could already sense the chasm growing between them as wide as the worlds they talked about. So she slapped him playfully and said, "You lie!"

~~~

She was right and she was wrong. When he won his scholarship to Canada, she was happy for him but couldn't meet his eyes for days. He would stroll in and tell Mama all about the place he was going to study. Alberta, they called it. He spoke of beautiful mountains he couldn't wait to go visit. This one day, he kept talking and talking, hoping for her to meet his eyes. Finally, Mama said to him,

"You for stop now. Go na de back door. She go come meet you."

They both froze—They had no idea Mama knew about their meet-ups! He finally found his feet and rushed on outside. Mama turned to her, reverting to proper Krio and said:

"Good luck don falla am—you for glady for am. Some tem you nor go see am again, but na dat make you for go tell am goodbye."

He's received good fortune. Be happy for him. You may never see him again so that's why you should say goodbye

Mama turned back to her cooking, cutting okra as if nothing had happened. She finished the peanut paste she was pounding, set it next to Mama and went out to meet him.

They leaned against a tree, holding each other loosely. The intensity as they drank in each other's eyes said it all. They would miss each other's company, friendship and the thrill of their secrecy. They made no promises. When it was time to go, they walked back slowly, holding hands. At the gates, they said goodbye and each walked away without looking back. Two years later, she would hear her name and look up to see him there. She was pounding peanuts, just like that last day when they said goodbye. He smiled, taking in her eyes that welled up to her shock and shame. He said simply:
~~~

"I told you I would not leave you here to cook forever."

A Justice of the Peace proclaimed them married, and a year afterwards, she was on a plane on Christmas eve to join him. She had the ridiculous blanket coat he'd left for her to wear when she got to London and when she arrived in the place called Alberta.

~~~

Her eyes stung from the white glare of the snow. The chill cut to her bones. She couldn't get warm no matter how close to the fireplace she sat. He kept saying she would get used to it, but she didn't. He had talked of beautiful mountains but not of this freezing cold. She now understood why he'd given her the coat and she wouldn't take it off even in the house. At first, he was patient. Then one day they went to visit a friend of his. She refused to take the coat off at the friend's house and he looked irritated. The wife was nice but too eager to find out all about *Africa* and asked her funny questions like how far she had to walk to go to school. She hadn't gone to school, but even if she had, she would have taken transport. She didn't understand where the woman got her information and why she wouldn't stop asking questions. It was tiring, so after a while, she got tight-lipped. The men meanwhile, kept discussing things of learning. She fell asleep on the chair. When she woke up, her eyes met his glare and that was the last time he looked into her eyes to hear her soul. His eyes kept getting darker when set in her direction and seemed to be brewing a storm rolling in to crash into her.

He asked her to enrol in school. She said that wasn't why she had married him and come to this dreadful place. She wanted to be his wife, listen to his stories, cook him meals and have his babies…and she wanted to be warm again, she said. So no, she wasn't ready to go to school. She would learn English in a few months, she said, so she'd get better at speaking and reading it. But school—maybe later. The storm grew darker. It was after that she realised he stopped taking her to his friends' events and he stopped telling her about what he was learning. They began to coexist. His only words to her were his harsh attempts to make her conform to his ways and this world she wasn't sure she wanted. He reached for
~~~

her only in the darkest of the night. His movements were choppy and hurried, pushing the cold from her bones to her heart.

~~~

She met a friend at the Walmart a block from their apartment. They had connected in a way only foreigners in a new land can. Azam was stocking shelves but stopped to come over and help her when she saw her looking bewildered in front of the bread section. Eventually, it was Azam who explained why there were so many of the same items and the idea of different brands competing for her money. Azam helped her figure out how to use coupons and showed her how to maximise her money by buying on sale. Azam was as foreign as she was, but she certainly knew her way around. Azam helped her get a job cleaning the store and stocking shelves at night.

He didn't realise she had been working for 2 weeks—he had taken to sleeping at a friend's house, he said, to study during exams. He was livid when he found out. How dare she do such a thing without telling him? She didn't tell him Azam had helped her read the papers and explained her social insurance number card to her. She told him she'd taken her whole bundle of identification cards to the supervisor who had copied what he needed and given her the package back. He demanded all her documents that day. She handed them to him—watching as he placed them in the small home safe and memorizing his lock combination. He also didn't know that Azam had already helped her enrol in English as a Second Language classes. ESL classes, that required rite of passage for non-English speaking or non-western-educated immigrants. She was learning how to read and write and making more friends who understood her. The storm motivated her. The more she learned, the more she realised she could beat the storm before it caught up with her.

After a while, Azam was also becoming irritated with her. *Why do you call him Baba! He has a name, you know! Why do you let him treat you like this? You are not his servant; you are his wife!* Azam had been helpful to her, so she tolerated the complaining. She asked how calling her husband *Baba* was different from Azam calling her own *Honey* on the phone. Azam tried explaining, but it didn't make sense, so she stopped listening.
~~~

~~~

My name is Safie. I have told you this story for you to see how good my English has become. On the day my Baba yelled at me for peeling onto the chopping board, I left. While he was in the bathroom, I opened the safe and took my papers. I also took all the money he had in there, including all his American dollars. I put them into the backpack I took to work along with a few things. His words and actions were chopping me away slowly. I started having a recurring dream, that the storm boils over and he beats me until I disappear in a red pulp into the soil I hail from. The chasm between us had become continents and oceans wide. He wanted this place, this life in Edmonton, Alberta and beyond, more than he wanted me. I realise now that the light I used to see in his eyes was his vision of the life he wanted. Now that he had that life, there was no need for me, because I didn't fit the landscape. He had no place where he could neatly fit me if I wouldn't run across the chasm to him before he walked away. I couldn't wait for him to finish chopping me.

I did chop a piece of myself—sacrificed to him that day as an offering for my sanity. As I was leaving, the baby who never cried started screaming. The baby knew. The baby was 18 months then and was the only reason Baba came home on the nights I had to work. I told myself I wouldn't have left if the baby was a girl, but he was a boy and he would survive because Baba will teach him about this world. I knew by then that in this world, baby will be an adult at 18 and free to find me. He is now almost 13. He is so handsome. I know he is well because I have been back to watch him walk to and from school. I was there today and another new Aunty greeted him when he unlocked their house door. The Aunties had one thing in common. They are all very different than me because they and their people have been here for a few generations.

It was Azam who I drove to Vancouver with the morning after our night shift. Azam has relatives here and drives back and forth most long weekends. I have stayed because of the year-round warmer weather. I am no longer cold all the time and my heart too, has started to thaw. I am working and almost done studying nursing. I even know more than Azam these days. Who knows, I may even do
~~~

more schooling afterwards. Mama still blames me for leaving. She cries every time I call—*what kind of woman leaves her husband, AND her child!* She will not relent, not even after I explained it all and told her my Baba never came looking for me even though he knew where I was. He knew, because he sent me the divorce papers to sign exactly a year to the day that I left. The papers said the divorce was on grounds of desertion. After the lawyer at the new immigrants' program explained it to me, I signed the papers, but scratched out desertion and wrote beside it in bold red letters: ***CHOPPED!***

So, for now, I count the days and years and pray every day. I pray that baby will listen to me when we meet and understand why I left. I know he will believe me when I tell him, because he was there. He felt the storm rolling in as surely as I did. That's why he was looking at Baba from his highchair and screaming as I stood at the door watching one last time before I left. My Baba had gone back over to the chopping board. The last sounds I heard as I closed the door softly, apart from baby crying, were a few furious bangs landing on the chopping board: C*hop! Chop! Chop!* I had wondered how long it will take Baba in the morning to realise I had left.

~~~

Tom leaned against the front door. He looked around, breathing in deeply the memories of this place. He breathed out and willed himself strength for the task ahead. His feet finally moved his body. He felt stilted, robotic, but thankful that his body seemed to know what to do because his mind was foggy. He found himself touching the grand piano, letting his fingers run through the keys.

"Come on son, there's middle C.

"Yeah, yeah that's it!!!"

He could hear the sounds of ♪jingle bells♪ floating through the room and see his Pops yelping in celebration of his novice victory of getting through the score in one go. He sat in his spot, then placed his hand where the old man would have been beside him. He imagined the seat was warm to the touch and the memories brought a smile.
~~~

♪Oh what fun it is to ride in a one-horse open sleigh♪

"That's my boy!"

He played the keys now but pressure started building in his foggy mind so he stopped, standing up and flipping the piano cover closed. The slam of the cover sounded louder than he had intended, startling him and reminding him of the emptiness of the space.

He continued to meander through the room, walking into the living room and leaning against the door post. He looked across at the giant oak book shelf that was ceiling high and laughed out loud, causing an echo through the space. A sprinkle of fine dust floated into the air from the vibrations.

"Pops, Pops look at me! I climbed all the way up!"

His Pops was standing where he now leaned, and he had never seen the man look so horrified.

"Get down, right now son!"

"Ok" He'd answered, and promptly jumped from the top of the bookshelf, landing with a large thump on the floor and moving into a superman pose, a triumphant smile adorning his face.

Pops had implored him not to fly off the furniture but then he realised that the superhero phase had only just begun. All Tom wore was superhero outfits. Superman was his favourite, complete with his cape. Then Tom came home one day to find the whole house jump-proofed. The beloved ceiling-high bookcase that he had perfected scaling at super speed had a huge clear furniture cover over it. Tom had flopped down in front of it and cried. Pops completely ignored the tantrum.

Now, Tom walked over and picked up the framed picture of him and Pops that adorned the centre of the bookshelf. The two of them at his high school graduation. They looked so happy. Pops looked so proud and Tom thought he looked—well awkward. He grimaced at the teenage image of himself. Pimply. Lanky. His jawline and shoulders were just starting to transition to the sculpted lines of manhood. It was like the image of an unfinished painting with all the basic lines formed, but at the stage where the artist is deciding what kind of portrait the final should be. Where to add shadow and light, softer lines and stronger angles. He couldn't believe that was already 25 years ago.

The scene from the weeks leading up to that graduation started to replay. He needed the usual throwback pictures for the graduation class video. A baby picture, first day of kindergarten, a fun candid shot.

"How about this one?"

"Oh no!! No naked bath pictures!"

They were laughing together, going through his photo box of baby pictures and keepsakes.

"I think I'll take this one."

It was a picture from Walmart Photo Centre of a chubby baby Tom, adorned with the grin of his first tooth, wearing only a diaper and a sailor's cap.

"hmm—why not the nicer portrait ones from your first birthday taken by Canadian Baby Photographers. They are more professionally done…"

"No" Tom interjected. *"too formal. I like this one."*

Pops tried a bit longer to convince him but finally gave up.

"Ok buddy. Let's pack up. We need to be up for hockey practice in the morning"

"Right…" Tom had considered asking for a pass. The 4:00 a.m. hockey practice mornings were brutal for him, but Pops was so committed and it was league time. Tom had decided to just keep going and finish that league, but he had no intention of continuing on with hockey once he went to college. He would much rather be playing soccer or basketball but every time he broached the topic Pops had simply looked at him and said.

"Don't be stereotypical." Or *"We live here, hockey is much more important."*

Tom had dropped it after a few tries.

They started packing the pictures away. Tom remembers bantering about their day. With the photo box all packed, Tom lifted it into its spot in the wall cabinet and turned to leave.

Crash!

They both groaned at the same time, starring despondently at the spill of photos all over the floor in front of them. They had been sorted in the box by age progression but the dividers had popped out and the photos were all mixed up.

"Sorry Pops! You go on to bed, I'll repack them."

"It's ok, son. Four hands are better than two. Let me help you. It was an accident but I need water so I'll grab a bottle—want one?"

"Sure! Thanks."

Pops went off and when he came back, Tom was sitting cross-legged in the middle of the photos, an envelope in his lap, flipping through the pictures in his hand.

"I found this sticking out of the lining at the bottom of the box, Pops. These pictures—they are of my mom, right?"

Pops had first looked sheepish, then angry. It was a quick switch. Like dark clouds rolling quickly in over a blue sky. It scared Tom because Pops never got that way with him although he had seen him get that way with the Aunties, usually just before they leave and Tom never sees them again.

"You should put those away."

Tom had hesitated, ready to comply like he always did. Pops had always been a good father, so Tom felt like he owed him the perfection he required. He loved seeing Pops happy and hearing him say: *"that's my boy!"*

But that day Tom's heart started pounding faster. He needed to know, so he pressed on.

"I also found a birth certificate. It has my birthdate on it, your name as father and lists Safie Conteh as mother. What I'm confused by is my name is listed as

OrThaim here, not Tom…and you are Robert Koroma, not King"

Pops' face now looked like a storm.

He closed the space between them in what seemed like one quick move and snatched the envelope.

"Your name is Tom! How are you supposed to live in this place, saddled with a name like OrThaim, huh! Tell me. As soon as people hear it, they want to know where it's from and what it means! Then we say Chief and it's downhill from there…."

Tom had quietly answered: *"I don't mind having a different name, Pops. And I want to know about my mother. Where is she? Did she die?"*

"She's dead to me. She stole from me and deserted you. Hand me that birth certificate." His voice signalled finality.

Tom handed Pops the birth certificate. He put it back into the envelope and returned the envelope underneath the photo box lining. They repacked the rest of the box in silence. The next day after school, Tom went straight to the photo box, pulled out all the photos and lifted the lining. The envelope was gone. Tom shuddered thinking about all the time he spent going through Pops' drawers hoping to find that envelope. He never did and he was convinced Pops got rid of it. When he was going away to university and asked for his documents, Pops handed him a different envelope. In it was a certificate of name change and a reissued birth certificate dated for 2 years' after he was born.

Tom set the graduation picture back down and started fingering the spines of Pops' favourite books. Classics in History, Philosophy and Politics lined the shelves—Descartes, Hegel, Jean-Paul Sartre, Friedrich Nietzsche, Sun Tzu, Nicolo Machiavelli and endless geology and geography books…Tom groaned. His book shelf looked so different. It was another point of departure for them. Before the photo box incident, Pops had walked into his room one day to find him reading *Black Berry, Sweet Juice: On Being Black and White in Canada.* He'd asked Tom:

"Why are you reading that?"

Tom answered: *"well—I identify with his experiences a lot… I mean, we don't even have a black barber in this city…"*

Pops had interjected: *"That's just the reality of where we live, nothing to dwell on. You shouldn't focus on those things."*

After the photo box incident, Tom made sure Pops didn't catch him reading Uncle Tom's Cabin or see him working on his assignment for Socials—a self-selected book review of Canada's Forgotten Slaves: Two Hundred Years of Bondage. He had learned how to abate and take cover from the storm.

Tom sighed and took a deep breath. He realised he needed to stop avoiding what he needed to do. The packers and movers will take care of all the furniture and everything else he leaves behind, but he needed to sort through all Pops' paperwork and personal effects today. It was going to be a long day. He decided to start in the master bedroom, then his old bedroom and then back down here to the book shelf. He may keep and finally read one of two of the classic philosophy books. Tom made his way upstairs, flooded with images of sliding down the banister. He paused to take in the photos that lined the way upstairs, making mental notes of the ones he would keep. He smiled again, noticing how much the images of him on the walls matched his fathers' ideals and not his life.

There were pictures from his hockey days, graduations and pictures of him in suits from his brief stint in the corporate world or at events that required him to wear one. They were mostly of times when he was out with his father and his latest girlfriend and their family and friends. They were inevitably well-connected or politically inclined, the monied mining establishment, conservative, philosophically-oriented and not Black. He was clean-shaven and close cropped in nearly all of them. In his reality that started at college, Tom's friends, who were multicultural and diverse, called him OrThaim. He wore his hair in a small afro. He generally dated girls who were feminist, multiracial, and loved talking about solutions to racial issues and black consciousness. He never brought any of them home. He wore African print shirts bought at one of a few African stores that had cropped up in town. He used to stare at the women in those stores because they looked like the woman in the picture whose face was sheered into his memory. She had a shiny dark chocolate hue, with large kind eyes and a square jawbone like his own. When he closed his eyes, he could picture her looking kindly at him and could almost feel her hands on his skin. In the picture Pops snatched from him that night, she was wearing a headwrap and a winter coat, looking both beautiful and confused.

Tom laughed out loud at the last picture at the top of the stairs. It was of him receiving a top-performer recognition and bonus at his junior account executive job. He quit within 3 months of that and started a chain of barber shops and the finest high-end African imports stores which became franchises across Canada. Pops never talked to him about his 'new' work and simply told his friends that Tom was CEO of his organisation. Tom would smile and talk about how his work involved supporting community youth to develop business skills and open their own franchises. He would then smile and nod at the comments about how noble and lovely that must be for him. He didn't tell Pops that his friends' wives were the largest growing clientele for his high-end art and his *Made in Africa: Ageless Beauty Secrets* products and services. Some of them he'd have already met as clients before meeting them at events with Pops and they either pretended or didn't actually recognise him.

In Pops' bedroom, Tom quickly got through the closet. He was broader-framed than pops but they both hovered around 6 feet. He only wanted a few shirts, one suit and any pair of pants that he could wear well with his African print shirts. He sorted through ties, then looked through the accessories box and decided to just take it all —cufflinks, an amazing watch collection and an assortment of gold and silver jewellery. Tom found a wedding band at the bottom of the box. He fingered it, saddened. He decided there and then he wouldn't use that ring.

Tom found the fireproof safe at the back of the closet as he'd been instructed. Pops had left the keys with his lawyers along with his will. Tom sighed, thinking about the simplicity of the will. Pops had left all his worldly possessions to Tom, his only listed family filled out on the family tree tool the lawyer provided. His wealth consisted of the house and two investments that had done fairly well and these personal effects. The only special instructions were that Tom was to annually transfer a portion of the dividends yielded from one of his investment portfolios to someone who lived in Njala, Sierra Leone. There was a name—Moses Koroma—a phone number and an email address for communicating when the money was sent. In the relationship box, Pops had noted: "a distant relative and the custodian of the ancestral family affairs."

Pops had noted that Tom was only to send the annual amount no matter what requests were made to the email address. Further, he was to ensure he established contact before sending the amount but was to stop the payments if he was unable to reach Moses or received news that he had passed away. Tom grimaced at the thought that the totality of a man's life had come to this. He had loved Pops and Pops had loved and cared for him well. He was grateful for that, but somehow Pops had locked himself in an isolation cell of his own making. At the end, he had become a prisoner of his own philosophies and lost in his imaginations of the places he had visited physically or mentally to observe rock and volcanic formations or speak about geological technicalities to mining moguls. Pops' funeral had a decent turnout, but it was a gathering of strangers who Tom had felt no real connection to. There wasn't even an Aunty by his side in the end.

Tom braced himself for the task of going through the papers. An hour later, the pile he had completed was only a sliver of what was left. He considered stopping to call Teuila, then decided he would wait till he was finished to stay focused. He was already distracted thinking about her. They had connected instantly at a dinner party hosted by a mutual Senegalese friend, Njie. It was a core gathering of French West Africans and their friends from all over the world. The food had been amazing: jollof rice, chicken yassa, white rice and maafe. Tom was slowly dabbling into West African food products so he had supplied imported cases of palm wine for the party. He'd been instantly drawn to her, but she was stuck talking and dancing with this guy Youssef to the mix of Mbalax, Soukous and Afrobeat music. Youssef eventually went to the toilet and Tom made his way to introduce himself. He was lost the moment he reached her and she stretched out her hand, eyes sparkling and said: "Hi, I'm Teuila, pronounced Ta-wee-lah. I'm an island girl of Polynesian and Jamaican descent. Youssef's fiancé is my bestie but she's home sick so I'm his plus one tonight. How about you? What's your descent and how did you get to this party?"

Her beauty was distracting, but her confidence was his magnet. As soon as he said he was of Sierra Leonean descent she exclaimed: "Oh! My dad was a Jamaican Maroon! We may have ancestral connection." Her dad had served in the American army and while stationed in Hawaii had met her mom, who was of Tahiti/French Polynesian and Fijian descent. He was a casualty of the Afghanistan war. Tom and Teuila hit it off and he ended up driving her home and walking away with her number. The next day, he sent a simple message: "can I take you to dinner?" She replied: "yes." That was 5 years ago. They'd been inseparable since. He was pretty certain she was the one. He planned to ask her to marry him one of these days.

With Teuila on his mind he decided to push through. The sooner he got out of there, the sooner they could get together. Maybe they will order dinner in and watch a Netflix series tonight. He opened the next envelope. Car insurance papers. Perfect—the car was already at the dealership, listed for sale. Or maybe they'd go check out the new Ethiopian restaurant. Or the lounge with Mediterranean food, belly dancers and live music. Investment banker details. He wondered what she was doing right now. Pulled out an envelope. She should be heading home. Flipped through some legal papers absentmindedly…

~~desertion~~ ***CHOPPED!***

His starred at the bolded letters in red. It took a few seconds before his mind could comprehend what he was looking at. He flipped to the front, then flipped back to the signatory page. It was signed by Pops and by Safie Conteh.

~~~

OrThaim and Teuila sat on their porch enjoying the brilliant sunset. There was a light harmattan breeze blowing as they swung gently along in their double bamboo hammock chair. This was their loveseat. This place their paradise. The sun was glimmering on the waters that were fading into a dark blue-grey as the sun descended. The waves crashed on the shores as the tide came in, looking like double layers of whipped cream where they met the sands on the seashore. The sun lowered further, painting the whole scene red. All those walking on the beach became silhouettes in the distance.

"Gosh it's beautiful!" Teuila exclaimed.

OrThaim squeezed her shoulder to acknowledge her words with his hand that had been laying lazily there while he read from his tablet. She snuggled a bit closer into his shoulder. He dropped his hand down to rub her bulging belly, his new favourite pastime. She smiled into his shoulder blade and laid her hand on top of his, twirling his wedding ring. They had had it locally made.

The dogs started barking. OrThaim looked up to see Grandma Phebe walking in through the side gate joining the houses in the compound he had built. The dogs settled down when they saw her.

"Una Kushe. Una alright? Una don ready for eat?"
~~~

Greetings. Are you two alright? Are you ready to eat?

They both looked up smiling as Grandma approached to greet them. They returned her hugs and Teuila answered:

"Not yet Grandma. I'm still belly-full from the peanut soup lunch."

Grandma Marie laughed – "No to peanut soup, say grannat soup"

"Grannat soup." Teuila replied with a grin. Grandma was teaching her Krio. Peanuts were *grannat.*

Grandma sat across from them, taking them in.

"Ar go miss una. Una take tem na road, ya."

I will miss you. Safe Travels

OrThaim put his tablet down, stood up slowly to make sure Teuila didn't get rocked too fast, then went over to Grandma. He sat in front of her and she cupped his face the way she loved to. She had lost a bit of her eyesight after multiple cataract surgeries, but what she'd lost in sight she made up for with touch.

"We go cam back quick quick. Nor worry. As de baby able travel, we go cam. This is home now." He said.

We will be back as quickly as the baby can travel.

"By God Power" Grandma replied. "You fiba you Mama."

You look like your mom.

The inevitable words Grandma said every time she held his face.

OrThaim smiled a bittersweet smile. A tear ran down each eye. He smiled, letting them fall. One for the sorrow of all he had missed and one for the joy of what looking for Safie had given him. All this, as well as connection to Pops' family via Moses Koroma.

That day he found his parents' divorce agreement, he lost it. What did she mean by chopped? He had called Teuila. Unhinged. Ranting. She was an hour away and kept him on the phone while she jumped in her car to drive to him. Along the way she'd asked:

"What else is in the envelope?"

Only then did he look to find a handwritten card that read.

> *Baba,*
>
> *My conscience is clear in why I decided to leave. You can tell the story your own way but a long time ago you stopped listening to my story. I did not desert you and OrThaim, but I know you enough to know you would never let me take him. I am sending you a copy of the essay I wrote in the English Writing class I've been taking. Perhaps you may understand what I mean by chopped.*
>
> *I wish you a great life and I am praying my son will choose to find me one day.*
>
> *I did love you once.*
>
> *Safie*
>
> *P.S. You can stop your private investigator from following me around now that we are divorced. If you need to ever reach me for baby's sake, please see my Vancouver number below. If you can't reach me, please contact Azam. I will always make sure she knows where I am.*

Azam had picked up on the first ring.

> *You are who. Slow down. I can't hear you. Ahhhhhhhhhhhhhhhhhhhhhh. You are Safie's son!! Yes, I know who you are, OrThaim. Your mom isn't picking up because she has left Vancouver. [long pause]. Yes, I am still here. [tears in her voice]. Your mom has been longing for this day. She did look for you before she left but we couldn't find you online or anyway. There was no forwarding address for your dad's last home either. Oh! OK. Ah! You go by Tom King! No wonder we couldn't find you! Your mom – she went back to Sierra Leone. I have her numbers, but I would advise that you don't call her now. She may not be able to handle it from a distance. You must go to her as fast as you can…*

It took two weeks to get all his paperwork together and get the vaccines he needed. They were the longest two weeks of his life. Azam wouldn't say more than that Safie was not ok. Every day, he agonised about whether to call, but he heeded Azam and Teuila and connected with his mom's cousin instead. She agreed with the others. She thought it best for him to arrive instead of contacting Safie before. She would make the arrangements to pick him up at Lungi International Airport and get him to Safie. She was staying with her mom in Sussex Village on the Freetown peninsula where she had grown up. Aunty sent a picture of her to get him through. The picture he received showed a mature version of the picture he had seen with Pops. Where there had been a headwrap, she had cornrows that showed off her beauty even more. She had the same kind eyes, but her face was much leaner. That picture got him through.

~~~

When Safie was told she had a visitor, she expected one of her girlfriends or relatives who had heard she was home. Her days were so much better since she came back. She loved visiting with people unless she was feeling too ill or nauseated and she loved the work she'd been able to do training health educators across the country. She was happier than she had been in years. Her only burden continued to be the heartache that she had lost her son in Canada. She had started making her peace with the reality that she would never see him again in this life. She thought of it as the cross she had to bear for the life she had created for herself. When she stepped out that day and saw him, her world stopped. He didn't have to say a word. They simply flew into each other's' arms. The household members were wise enough to quickly bring them chairs. She crashed into hers and he laid his head on her lap, where she rocked him as they both cried. She repeated over and over again, "My son, my baby. My son, My baby…"

He learned that she had eventually become a Registered Nurse, working in Oncology. So when she got the breast cancer, she knew what to expect. Early detection and the best Canadian health care had saved her the first time. But when it came back aggressively, she decided she would not do any radiation or chemotherapy anymore. She was close to retirement and had lived a good life. She
~~~

would rather be as healthy as she could until the end and contribute to cancer sensitization and education, a dire need in these parts. She had spent the past year doing that. At first, she felt that the change in weather and being back surrounded by family gave her a boost, but by the time her baby found her, the weight loss, nausea and shortness of breath had accelerated.

OrThaim has asked Teuila to join him. They got married within the month of her arrival. Safie could barely stand more than 10 minutes by then but she was radiant. Three weeks later, she said goodbye to them. She held their hands on either side of her, while Grandma Phebe mopped her balmy forehead, singing softly through her tears, the song Safie had told her was her favourite memory of their times in the kitchen when she was in Canada:

> *Leh we cook for dem pikin dem. Tell God tenke for provision! For provision, for provision, tell God tenke for provision!*
>
> *Safie dey learn for cook for im pikin dem, leh we show am how for cook. Leh we show am how for cook, how for cook, how for cook, leh we show am how for cook!*
>
> *Safie go train im pikin for cook…leh e learn how e go train am. How e go train am, how e go train am, leh e learn how e go train am!*

~~~

Grandma Phebe picked up the incoming WhatsApp call.

"Na girl!" OrThaim screamed. "We named her Safie Mabone Phebe Koroma."

It's a girl!

"Ahhhh" Grandma screamed. "God be praiseddddddd!!!"

"Safie en namesake, Me namesake, Mabone oh Mabone!!!

Safie's namesake, my namesake. Joy, oh joy indeed!!!!"

~~~

3. LEGACY

The secretary smiled sympathetically. That's when Neema realised she was slouched and biting her nails. She sat up straight, offered a smile back and folded her hands neatly in her lap. The secretary looked away quickly, as if she was sorry for their silent exchange. Neema didn't blame her. She must have seen many a desperate hopeful like herself. The blanket of self-pity and shame covered her. It was becoming a familiar sensation. She was slouching again. Her confidence had seeped away fifty audition interviews ago and she was working hard to gain it back.

> *"Remember, show presence! Watch your posture!"* Her mom's ever-present voice said.

She sat up once more. Scanned herself again. *Shoot!* There was a small ketchup stain on her skirt from her hasty MacDonald's meal on the way here. And her nail polish on her left index finger was chipped. She would have to remember to keep her hands folded in her lap over the ketchup spot to hide both these imperfections. No talking with hands today.

"Ms. Bangurah?"

She stood and walked in after the secretary. The sequence was the same as always. Stern faces. Hot lights. An expressive reading. A dance routine. We'll let you know. Ushered out through the back door. Today's was all over in 3 minutes and 20 seconds. It felt like the worst kind of one-night stand. Melancholy swept over her as she walked out of the building.

"Just study hard," her mother said. *"We made these sacrifices for you so you can do whatever you want with your future."*

Her dad never said very much. He was a qualified doctor driving a transit bus in this place and he was tired of saying that. He didn't want to hear the one-liners anymore:

"Imagine what your life would have been like if you'd stayed there!"

"What! That's outrageous!"

"Have you done all the exams? Applied for all the residences?"

He was simply tired of explaining that yes, he'd done all that, tried all that, and had now given up for the sake of providing for his family. Neema watched how his shoulders would slump under the weight of his wife's words every time she told the children they would do better. Neema tried to avoid his eyes in those moments, so he wouldn't see her pity too. She used to think he was too much of a pessimist and had brought it on himself for giving up so easy in their name. She only just began to understand when she decided not to go to medical school, or finish her science degree even though she was a straight A student. As she walked away from audition number one hundred five that day, her shoulders also slumped, just like his used to.

Her sister Suraya who wasn't as good as she was in sciences went to medical school. She was the goody-two-shoes, determined to fulfil their parents' dreams. She never tried cigarettes or drank underage. She said her devotionals at night and spent extra time at the library. Neema didn't understand her dedication to studying because she only ever did average. One day, she woke up and it was Suraya's medical school graduation day. She could hardly believe it. What Neema remembers most about the graduation though, is that the light returned to her father's eyes that day.

Two years after that, she joined the family again for her brother Tariq's law school graduation. Her father was as quiet as ever, but the light in his eyes was even brighter. That was the first day she felt the blanket of shame cover her. Till then, she was simply following her own path. Doing her own thing.

> *"Neema look at the honour you denied us! You are the eldest and we never got to see your graduation! How could you not tell us! This is what we worked for and God answered!"*

Neema had laughed and looked away. Suraya had looked at her accusingly, saying with her eyes, *you should tell them.* Neema's eyes replied back: *none of your business.*

"I registered for graduation too late, Mama," she had said with a smile.

That part was true. She did not attend her graduation from the fine arts program which she'd transferred into after a year in Computer Sciences. Coding came easy to her, but it bored her to her soul. She knew her parents wouldn't understand or accept her doing anything less than the big five every parent in their circles demanded of their children—The STEM professions of science, engineering, technology or math, economics or accounting, law, medicine or a university professor. Or something with bragging rights like becoming a pilot, or being the first of something. Like a major cable news anchor like Isha Sesay of BBC, then CNN. Or Michaëlle Jean, Journalist turned Canadian Governor General. Neema knew she would cause them sore disappointment if they knew what her life was really like, especially with her science smarts. She got gigs at the local theatre and had started teaching children's classes there, but she had yet to land the Broadway show that would make them proud and free her from living her lies.

She only had enough time to change into her server's outfit when she got home. She raced back out to the pub and lounge, getting there just in time to start her shift. It was a busy night. She did well in tips as always. And as always, some tips came with the price of the flagellation of her soul through her mother's voice—her daily penance for chasing her own dreams.

"Wanna quit this job and come work for me instead," one said, slipping her a $100 bill.

> *"Imagine! Blessing's daughter, Ashawo life! Bartending at the pub Shhhhh!"*

"I could give you a much bigger tip if you serve me only, brown sugar." This one, passing a $50.

> *"This second-class citizen lifestyle is not for us! We have to show them when we come here, we can do even better!"*

"I'll give you $20 now and more later." This, delivered with the wink and wrist grab.

> *"Ah! We did NOT come here to be anyone's servant! When you do those basic jobs, they will always take you less!"*

And the lewdest ones were always the cheapest.

When she got home, she scrubbed under the hottest water she could manage. Washing off their words and her shame. She usually had a cup of tea but the shame blanket shrouded her mind, causing her head to throb and making everything dark and fuzzy. She went straight to bed. The next morning when the alarm sounded, she turned it off, put the phone on silent and stayed in bed. She had another audition number waiting for her in a line-up somewhere downtown, but she didn't care. She would not be missed. She would just be another no-show. She slept in fits and starts. She eventually got up. Peed. Headed back to bed. The flashing light on her phone annoyed her, so she reached to turn it off. *Too many flashes,* she thought. *Not usual.* She unlocked the phone and stared at the text message. There was a matching voicemail and a matching email. They all said she got the lead role in the off-Broadway musical, *The African.* That was her audition number ninety-eight from 4 weeks ago which she had submitted a video for.

In that moment:

Her mother said—

"By God's Grace we shall overcome!"

Her father's eyes projected the spotlight onto her from the front row special guest seating. And she thought:

What about every Papa and I who never get this call back?

She will take the part of course, but she will also use every spare moment to work on plays featuring people like her and her father. She decided she would send out a thousand scripts if she had to—until someone said yes. Mama applauded, same way she had when she told Neema to do the math test retake that Sue Wong had beat her on.

"You can be No.1. If you want it, you can do anything!"

~~~

"And the posthumous winner of the Global Theatre Legacy award is: Neema Bangurah."

Naisha's head exploded into a thousand pieces as her brain absorbed the announcement. For a few seconds that felt like forever, she couldn't hear anything and everyone around her seemed to be moving in slow motion. She heard the blood rushing to her ears and the throb of her own heartbeat before she heard the clapping. It was thunderous. All of it was surreal!

A grin exploded over her face and she found her feet. She would later think about the walk from her seat to the stage as the ancestral victory walk. There were bright lights, flashing cameras, handshakes and then she was handed the award—a golden statue of a black woman in motion, with a giant globe in her hands.
~~~

"Wow! Anyone here who knew my grandmother would know why this award is absolutely fitting for her! She never stopped. She worked tirelessly and her vision for the world of theatre and the world at large only got bigger as she aged. Today, I am a believer in her vision. Grandma was known only for her role in *The African*, the off-Broadway show that ran for a dozen years but never made it to Broadway. But today, I am holding this posthumous award on her behalf because of the money she left in trust to start the Global Theatre Foundation and because of her hit play: *Nirvana*, still running on Broadway and globally through the Foundation for its twentieth year!!"

There was thunderous applause.

"The Foundation and Nirvana represent her true passions. By the end of *The African*, Grandma was convinced that unless there was an international theatre organisation that rivalled Broadway and actively cultivated international talent, underrepresented voices and artists will remain marginal. '*We need to own the platforms not just work for them!*' She used to say. So, while her family chastised her for being a dreamer, she quietly put her plans into motion. After *The African*, she realised there was much more wealth in writing and producing so she became a prolific shadow writer and producer. I have just been told that the productions for which she was never named and never known are listed on the leaflet accompanying the award announcement and her biography"

By then, Naisha's voice was breaking. She paused, sipped from the glass of water that had been handed to her, and continued.

"My Grandmother lived modestly and invested as much of her money as she could, except for what she used to put my father, her only child, through the best boarding schools while she worked tirelessly. I became Grandma's companion and confidante when my mother passed away unexpectedly and my father's job meant he was always travelling. She wasn't as comfortable sending me to Boarding school as she did with my father, so she took me everywhere with her, with a nanny and tutor. I watched Grandma write and write and write. My bedtime stories were scripts when she was feeling stuck and wanted to hear the words out loud and get my childlike opinions. I learnt this business by osmosis, watching her, seeing what worked and what didn't. So when she read me *Nirvana*, we both knew it would be a hard sell. *Nirvana*, a world where there was no racial tension or prejudice and those seeking refuge never had to fear rejection. A world where people operated from primal love instead of primal fear. *Nirvana*, was ahead of its time. But Grandma knew and I knew that it was something special. The conviction in her voice that we all need a vision of *Nirvana* was clear. And it was clear she wasn't going to stop until that script and that message got out to the world. So, when Grandma passed away and left me all her scripts and writings that she never sold, I knew that if I only did one thing to honour her legacy, it would be to get *Nirvana* into the world."

Naisha paused, trying to hold back her emotions, but when Neema's smiling face flashed before her, she let the tears of joy fall.

"I am so so glad that I made the right deals with Broadway and that the Global Theatre Foundation agreed to spearhead taking the Nirvana production around the world! This, is the first award that my Grandma has ever received! Forty years after she wrote Nirvana and 25 years after her death! Grandma, it's happening—we are getting closer to Nirvana. Rest well Grandma!"

The two-minute warning flash went up. Naisha smiled through her tears, nodded to the production crew staff and continued:

"But the most important hero here today isn't Grandma. It's my Great Grandfather. My refugee and immigrant great-grandfather, whose life inspired Grandma more than anything. My great-grandfather drove a bus in this land to care for his family because he gave up on trying to break into the system and work in his profession as a Medical Doctor. That was a choice so many in his generation made—the choice to live less than self-actualised lives as the sacrifice to lay a foundation of success for their children, grandchildren, and great-grandchildren. Great-Grandfather, I feel like I know you through Grandma's stories of you. So today, wherever you are in the universe of eternity, I know your eyes will be shining so brightly that I will be able to see them from here. I'll be looking for your star tonight. Thank you."

As Naisha turned to leave, there was a standing ovation. The

MC held her shoulders and motioned for her to stay.

"On behalf of the Foundation, we have one more presentation and announcement to make."

A hush fell over the standing crowd.

"To the millions watching all over the world, we want you to know that we, at the Global Theatre Foundation, hosts of these most prestigious Global Theatre Awards, believe in Neema Bangurah's vision of Nirvana and in the legacy she left behind. That is why we are renaming these Global Theatre Awards, to the Neema Awards effective immediately. And the first two Neema awards go to Neema Bangurah for the Legacy of Merit Award and Naisha Jones—please accept this Pioneer in Global Theatre Award."

The rest was a blur. Naisha remembered her husband joining her to help carry the awards. She remembered sobbing in what she would consider a less than dignified manner if the occasion had been different. She remembered watching the closing reel as it came up on screen—It was clips from *the African.* In the opening scene, a beautiful Neema runs onto the stage wearing an African print jacket over jeans, sneakers and an Ankara backpack. She faces off with her stereotypical media image counterpart, a traditional African, bare-chested and barefoot, ripe breasts oiled and wearing only a body wrap and a head scarf. Her enduring memory of the night was the collective gasp at the end of the reel at the picture of Neema and young Naisha at the finale of *the African.* Their heads were thrown back in laughter, with the poster of *the African* behind them. They were holding a script between them. The camera zoomed in to show the script they were holding was titled *Nirvana.*

As they drove home, Naisha asked her husband to stop by her Grandma Neema's grave. She stood by her tombstone, telling her how amazing the night had been. How proud she would have been. She placed all the awards on the tombstone and took a picture. She promised to come back and take another one in the daylight too. It was a clear night and as Naisha headed back to the car and her waiting husband, the brightest shooting star circled through the skies.

~~~

Sierra was feeling irritable. She was hot, sweaty and grumpy. This feeling happened every time she had to go into a live theatre showcase since she'd been on exchange in Freetown, Sierra Leone, at the Charlie Haffner School of Theatre and Fine Arts. It was the premier Theatre and Fine Arts school in the flourishing West African nation, previously known as the Athens of West Africa, now known as Africa's Cosmos Centre—a place of brilliance and light. This small West African nation was the land of her great great grandparents and somehow, they had insisted on leaving a breadcrumb trail to lead her back here. In fact, the breadcrumb trail was called a trust fund, and the only way she could access it in a year at age 21, was by doing this stupid one-year exchange program.

She had no intention of staying in the Arts or working anywhere near the Global Theatre Foundation where everyone in her family and all her aunts and cousins seemed to work, no matter their profession. It felt like the family pilgrimage and she found it stifling. If Grandma Naisha told one more Grandma Neema story at another family gathering, she had promised herself she would gag and throw-up!

Sierra groaned. *Why couldn't they just give me the money with no strings attached! Hell, she didn't even need to study or work for the rest of her life!*

"Little sista, you hungry?"

Brima, the driver and some distant relative, insisted on reminding her daily that they were related. It was his way of demanding higher status than the other drivers. That, and the fact that he preferred to speak English over Krio, even to the other staff who called him 'Or Portho' meaning white man for that reason.

Just then, her stomach growled.

"Ah, maybe you are right Brima, I am feeling hunger pangs now."

Hangry, that was it, she was hangry. Hungry. Angry. And nervous. These showcases were good. Gifted students came in from all over Africa every 3 months over the year to showcase the theatre
~~~

assignments they'd put together and she always felt that she didn't measure up. She wasn't happy with her previous ones and this was the finale. It was the only thing standing between her and the rest of her life.

She would rather be sleeping, dreaming about the amazing beach party she was at last night…and the gorgeous Prince she watched the sunset and spent the night with. She closed her eyes and smiled, thinking about the bright red sun sucking in the blue sky over glimmering waters, while the majestic mountains held court in the backdrop. Then she groaned. She wasn't completely hungover, but she had had a little too much of everything to drown out thoughts of the showcase. Food would help.

"Please can we stop by the Salone Snackables drive-through on the way to school?"

"Of course, little sister."

The traffic suddenly slowed and soon they were crawling and then stopped.

"Oh Lord!" Sierra exclaimed. "Not right now!"

They were at Lumley Circle and the traffic was heavier than usual this morning. Sierra had been told by Brima who doubled as her historian and tour guide that in the space between being named after Athens and the Cosmos, Sierra Leone had endured several tragedies that had stifled her development since independence from the British—a chain of coup d'états, civil war, an Ebola outbreak, a devastating mudslide. Sierra knew that her original immigrant ancestors had left because of the civil war. All the tragedies had led to internal displacements, overpopulation in the city, rapid deforestations and a non-existent urban planning scene. For a while, Brima said, the city struggled with overcrowding and noise pollution in areas that used to be residential. Tin shacks, small retail and large trading houses sprung up in the middle of everywhere. Brima said it was like the city was bursting at its seams as new communities seemingly encroached and took over old ones. Instead of developing, it had seemed that the city and her peoples were bringing new calamities on itself—from crippling traffic to public health challenges to daily accidents. Motor bikes and the three-wheeled motorised rickshaws, locally known as Keh Keh's had taken over the roads.

The famous Lumley roundabout was one of those areas that has been so affected, Brima told Sierra. Looking out the window now, it was hard to imagine. *Necessity is the mother of invention*, she thought. The view in front of Sierra was a ramp leading into a multilane traffic circle, with clear neon signage and a parallel Keh and bike lane. Those lanes were flowing freely and always busy as tourists were being taken either in the direction of Lumley Beach or underground for the Old Lumley experience. The Old Lumley experience included a museum, 24-hour music and talent shows, several 5-star 'street' restaurants, an amazing marketplace and a tour of the famous red cobbled-stone church that had adorned the corner of Lumley for generations. Only Keh Kehs and bikes operated in Old Lumley. It was a central tourist hub and always busy.

However, unlike Old Lumley, the new Lumley circle was usually free of daily traffic congestion and noise pollution. There was even a sound barrier between the two Lumley worlds. The sensory overload as soon as you cross the barrier into Old Lumley was part of its appeal and experience. It was hard to believe people had lived that way. The ingenious team of Sierra Leonean architects and urban planners who had worked on the new architecture of Freetown had accomplished the seemingly impossible. They now worked all over the world, creating sustainable cities on top of old ones that needed re-architecting.

The news screen in the Circle Centre flashed an update. Khadija, the traffic news robot announced that there had been a medical emergency in the tunnels leading to Old Lumley. Today, Khadija was wearing a fitted gara dress and headwrap. Sierra loved how Khadija showcased old and new Sierra Leonean and African fashion based on her constant searches through the old and new internets, with a sidebar showing the history of what she was wearing. Today's sidebar described the traditional west-African tie-dying process and industry by Sierra Leonean women before colonial times, when it became possible to imitate and manufacture the pattern and fabric in bulk. Yesterday, Khadija was wearing Dashiki print, which was only used in art and accessories now but apparently was dresswear in older generations.

"We apologise for the delay and disruption in your routine this morning, my people. All emergency responders are already onsite in the tunnel. Normal traffic flow will resume as soon as we have attended to the emergency."

"Oh, for crying out loud!" Sierra exclaimed, typing furiously into the Khadija news responder.

"How long will the delay be?" Sierra watched the screen to see that her question was the first one up.

"We expect the delay to only be another 15 minutes. My fellow robots are dispatching messages to all offices and schools noted with your registered vehicles; you will not be penalised for being late today."

"Everything happens for a reason" Brima offered "you will have extra time to prepare. And see—here comes Salone Snackable staff with food carts taking car orders and delivering food in traffic."

"Yaasssss!!" Sierra exclaimed.

A server pulled up to their window—Sierra ordered too much food; bread and olele, fried plantains, akara, fried fish and stew, dried oyster snacks, shrimps, a passionfruit milkshake.

Brima offered: "Little sister, the fridge in this car doesn't work so well. I'll be waiting a while when you are at showcase. The food will spoil in the heat."

"Right! Ok enough. Brima, you will have some too though, yeah."

"I already had breakfast but yes, I will make a small plate too"

Two minutes later their order was delivered. Sierra started eating when her phone alert went off.

Sierra, we have moved your showcase to the second set after the first break. Meanwhile, here is a live link. We start in 5 minutes. You can call in.

Ok thank you—Sierra

"Crap!" Sierra exclaimed "I can't do this!"

"Yes, you can, little sister. YOU are the legacy…the legend of our family says…"

"Not now Brima! Not now!"

Her head started pounding. She ate a handful of plantains. Rubbed her temples.

Legacy!

That was today's showcase theme.

"Sorry to snap, Brima. I'm just stressed. Ok—I'm logging into class now, so talk to you later!"

She didn't wait for a response before she put up the glass screen between them. She put on her virtual reality glasses, projected the link onto the screen and entered class.

It looked like only three of them were missing in action. Usually, most of the class, even those of them on location in Freetown joined class via their glasses, but showcase required live human performance. The head of their program was adamant—*theatre is theatre—it is best experienced between and with live humans.*

The countdown clock was ticking now: 10. 9. 8. 7. 6. 5. 4. 3. 2 and live!

"Welcome to your third showcase, *Legacy*. We have 18, ten-minute shows to experience, with a five-minute set-up transition for each. After each set of six performances, we will have a ten-minute break. It's an intensive five-hour run as you know, so buckle up for the ride. We've adjusted the line-up and may need to keep doing so depending on when Sierra, Antonia and Samba get here. In the meantime, the six in the first set are:

1. São Tomé and Príncipe: Maria Costa
2. Mauritania: Mohammed Aziz
3. Ghana: Sunday Owusu
4. Djibouti: Yasmin Farah

5. South Sudan: Zeinab Deng
6. Botswana: Baruti Kubisa

First up!"

Maria did a re-enactment of life as her ancestral mixed-race slave on a roças on a cocoa and coffee plantation in the midst of the beauty of Príncipe. Mohammed Aziz recaptured the experience of living in the unification period of the Arab-Berbers, Fulani, Soninke and Bambara through the eyes of a young Berber boy. His impressions of each ethnic group were flawless. Sunday's rendition of life as a diasporan returnee to Ghana during the 2019 Year of the returnee was an ode to the roots of thriving pan-Africanism and his ancestral grandparent who made the journey. He imagined the internal dialogues of Kwame Nkrumah and Nana Akufo-Addo on their journeys to leading the call across history.

Yasmin examined the global politics of the strategic Port of Djibouti at the entrance to the Suez Canal linking Europe, the Far East, the Horn of Africa and the Persian Gulf. Hers was told through the musings of a legendary Djibouti prostitute turned women's rights advocate and Nobel Laureate, who boarded the ships by night and brought down a sex slavery ring by filming evidence and posting it online in the days of WhatsApp. Zeinab traced her family's journey through the stages of the South Sudan wars, up to independence and beyond. Baruti Kubisa told the Botswana independence and Seretse Khama story, based on commentary over clips from the movie *A United Kingdom*, in the voice of various peoples of Bechuanaland.

The set was a brilliant blur. A trip through time, space, lineage, activisms and futurism on the continent. It stopped hearts at one turn, tore them at others and warped minds with the memories of the contradictions, outrages and love that had them arrive where they were today. *Legacy*. The stillness at the end of Baruti's showcase was broken with the announcement.

"That's a wrap of the first set in case y'all haven't noticed. We'll break for 10 minutes, then back to start right away with the second set. I understand Sierra has arrived and is waiting for break to come in so as not to disrupt—thank you Sierra. Set two is:

1. Sierra Williams, Sierra Leone…"

Sierra opened the car door and threw up. The red dust received her curdled yellow mash of plantains, olele, oysters, bread and bile, returning a splatter of it onto her shoes.

"Or Portho, you nor well?" *You unwell?*

Sierra looked up to meet the concerned eyes of a young boy and realised he meant her and not Brima. She was called Or Portho here as often as Brima—a recognition by strangers of her mixed lineage through the generations, given away by her wild curly afro, lighter brown skin and blue eyes. The boy was wearing the badge that identified him as a legitimate street guide. For families under the middle-income line, their young children were still allowed to work after school hours in Freetown, but only with the right identification, in safe public zones that had video surveillance robots. It was a major shift from the days of having children of poorer families drop out of school to roam as street hawkers, which had left girls vulnerable to sexual abuse and rape.

"Or Portho, hush ya…sorry. Can I help you with anything?" he said sympathetically, handing her a tissue.

"No, but thank you. I'm just going into the school," she answered.

"Little sista! Don't be so worried, huh! You will do us proud! You ARE the legacy!"

"BRIMA!" Sierra slammed the car door, narrowly missed stepping into her puke and rushed in.

She can never remember how she managed to get set up and put her make-up on. All she remembers is sitting on stage in the dark, listening to the promo reel and commentary for *Nirvana by Neema Bangurah* come on. She remembers the spotlight coming on as planned at the end of the reel. She remembers starting up in that projected version of her already gravelly voice that made it boom through silence and captivate audiences:

"Whose shoulders do you stand on? Where do you begin to tell your story in the endless chain of your ancestry? Who has left you legacy?..."

Then nothing.

Until the standing ovation that broke into the crescendo of her final scene, in which she finished her monologue of Papa Bangurah's musings from the grave, explaining why his star now shines so brightly it is mistaken for the moon. At the end, a picture sequence flickered through the storyline feature. The first was of Papa Bangurah, shoulders slumped in a winter jacket, eyes downcast beside his bus. It was a picture of a broken man. It faded into a picture of a family. Papa Bangurah. Mama Bangurah. Neema. Suraya. Tariq. Tariq was in a graduation hat and they were in a group hug. Papa Bangurah was laughing in the circle. His head was high—almost thrown back.

Sierra remembered leaving showcase, grabbing an astonished Brima and dancing with him. She remembered holding the glow of passing her last showcase for about two, maybe three months afterwards. She was pumped full of ideas, inspired by her own reflections on legacy and what her own had endured so that she could have a trust fund. But she also remembered being excited to leave at the end of her internship year. She regressed under the influence of the endless money she suddenly had access to. She lived the life she'd dreamt of, spending the next 20 years dining with the world's rich and famous in designer clothes, fast cars, private jets and chateaus, eating caviar and drinking champagne. Then she woke up on an island paradise resort with no memory of how she got there, or of how she ended up with the local stud in her room. She would send him away and wrapped in her designer robe, looking at the idyllic beach in front of her, she would remember her own Freetown paradise. She would relive her Legacy showcase and, in that moment, she wept.

Exactly 40 years from her showcase, Sierra walked through the doors of what used to be the Charlie Haffner School. It was the same site where she'd studied, but the building was expanded, shinier, newer, more equipped than it had ever been. It was a prime global education site for the arts, arts education and every technical and technology training under the sun for media production. Charlie Haffner's picture and story was still on the walls, but it was now The

Sierra School of Arts & Production. Sierra walked into a theatre hall and made her way to the front of a group of students and the production crew poised to start a showcase that she was to be part of judging. A hush fell over the room. Sierra scanned their faces and rested her gaze last on the darker-skinned mirror image of herself. They smiled at each other and Sierra marvelled at the sameness and difference between them. Her only daughter Leo was 16 going on 25 and had volunteered to help with every showcase production since she was ten. Leo will not need to be forced to do her exchange and in her case, she could do it anywhere globally.

Sierra felt a flood of emotion rising, but like every master performer, she held only enough of it to draw in her audience. She spoke, her gravelly boom laced with that soft underlying timbre that great storytellers perfect.

"Whose shoulders do you stand on? Where do you begin to tell your story in the endless chain of your ancestry? Who has left you legacy? My name is Sierra Mansaray, née Williams. I am here to tell you my story of legacy. I am here to tell you why I have gone around the world helping those seen as less-privileged and vulnerable to find their feet; why I do one-woman storytelling performances all over the world to inspire action in those who may be complacent in their privilege; why my home-base is here in Freetown; and why I support this industry. My story runs seven generations back from my daughter Leo…"

After she finished and stepped aside for the first set to be announced, she heard Brima, who passed away a year before saying:

Little sista, you have done well, huh! Thank you for doing us proud. You ARE the legacy!

She let her tears run.

4. FATIMA

My name is Fatima. When I was growing up, I never knew there was anything remarkable about my island. I didn't even know it was an island. It was just the place where I grew up, eating cocoyam and stew and scalping mango flesh so clean with my teeth, the seed would become as bald as the vultures that circled overhead as soon as there was a dead stray dog lying around. I woke up to the sound of breeze dancing with the trees and the swish of water against the shore line every morning, listening to the birds' chirp and watching the colour of the night change as the sunlight forced its way through the thick mud walls and the crevices of our thatch roof. I knew it was time to get up when the black darkness of a moonless night was chased out and the light in the hut turned silvery-yellow. But I liked to stay lying down, making out shapes that the dancing rays of light formed on the sides and floor of the hut. I would see shapes of birds, fishing boats, a mortar and pestle and all the different men, women and children of our town. I loved to see who the sun will show me in the morning. I knew that meant I would see them or encounter them that day.

I would lie there till I heard Grandma get up and hear the splash of water on the side of our hut which meant she was performing her ablutions for morning prayers. I would wait until she was done, then finally get up. By the time Grandma finished her morning prayers, I would have started the fire in our outside kitchen and heated a pot of water for her to wash and prepare our morning tea and cornmeal breakfast. I would have used up the last of our water for this, so then I'd start off to the water pumps. I would make three trips to fill buckets and two yellow five-gallon jugs. By the time I was finished with that, Grandma would be done with breakfast so I'd go to the back to greet her and eat together.

Mine was a simple life. It was just Grandma and I and, in those days, I didn't go to school. I don't remember my parents. I have heard that my mother fell ill with a terrible sickness soon after I was born. It is said that Pa did not even sleep in our hut the night she died. He simply buried her in the back and disappeared. I have heard Grandma say she is happy he at least left us a roof over our heads. I spent the days helping Grandma cook and tidy our hut and yard and collecting the herbs she used for making medicines and remedies. She taught me which barks are good for health and strength, which leaves to use for the tea that relieves headache and body pain and which root when boiled takes away the fever and heals malaria in two days.

After picking herbs, we would go to the market together. We would buy fresh and dried fish, peppers, onions, rice. And often lemons and some spices for mixing with Grandma's herbs. We would cook and eat lunch. Then in the evenings, people would come to see Grandma with their ailments and needs and she would give them herbs in exchange for money or provisions. This is how we earned our livelihood, for Grandma said she was too old to join the women who farmed alongside the men. She refused to send me even though some other young children went to the farm. She would not tell me why, except to say that she had lost everything and she would not lose me. When I got older, I realised Grandma did that to keep me away from the townsfolk and protect me. She was strong then and remained strong for a long time. We could have both gone farming.

In the evenings, when Grandma was seeing people, she would let me roam around and play in the beautiful woods around our hut. She did not want me hearing people's problems and stories, she said, because sometimes all the healing people needed was to talk. Grandma spoke Madingo, Fulani, Krio, Themne and some Mende. Even though I only spoke Themne and Krio, she knew I understood the other languages too so she would shoo me away. Grandma told me never to go past a certain point and I was forbidden from going to the stream in the woods or the beach shore on the other side of the hut. I mostly obeyed, but on days when there were people sitting on the benches waiting, I knew she would be busy till the moon returns to reclaim its place in the sky from the sun. By the time the last person left, I would be back just behind the hut and ready to answer when Grandma called that it was time to turn in.

On those busy days for Grandma, I would alternate between going to the stream or the beach shore to play mostly by myself. I was used to that. For some reason the townsfolk and children avoided me. For the children, I decided that it must be because when they played with me, they got in trouble. Take Hassan for example. He was the companion I found at the stream. The first time I met him, he was sitting on a rock, throwing pebbles into the stream. I turned to run away but he called out in Krio: "Mi padi! Nor run." *My friend! Don't run.* I was so surprised that someone called me a friend that I did as he bade. I stopped and walked back slowly, cautiously.

When I came out of the woods, I saw that he had the kindest face ever. His eyes smiled with his lips. He was standing, arm outstretched, offering me a pebble. I wondered if he was playing a trick but it was easy to believe him. I reached for the pebble, he pretended to snatch his hand back at the last minute but then gave it back, laughed and ran back to the rocks. We spent the next hour throwing pebbles at fishes and birds. He told me he had seen me come to the stream when he was up in the trees practicing tree climbing and had planned to meet me. I asked him why he wanted to do that when no one else wanted to. He said because I seemed like a girl who wouldn't be afraid to play with boys. When the sun started setting, I told him I had to go back. He grinned and said my secret was safe with him. I ran back just in time for Grandma's call.

Playing at the stream became our ritual. Until the day that his parents came looking for him. We were laughing so hard as we examined each other's private parts that we didn't hear them approach. We just heard Hassan's mother shriek. She reached for a tree branch shouting: "Witch! You don bewitch am! Witch!" I managed to escape before she could start hitting me with the branch she was waving manically over her head. I spent the next few days in fear, waiting for someone to come tell my Grandma about the incident. To this day, I don't know why no one did. Hassan and I would sneak quick waves at each other after that if an adult was not watching, but never spoke again until we were adults. Not too long after the incident, he moved to the mainland for school.

Another time, I met a group of girls at the beach. At first, they stared at me but didn't approach. I ignored them and kept playing, drawing shapes in the sand and mimicking the marks I found on the plastic bottles, cans and other debris that washed up on the shore. I did not yet know that they were letters spelling words in English, but I used to copy them out onto the sand.

C-O-K-E.

B-E-E-R.

PE-T-R-O-L-E-U-M.

The kids were still staring and whispering, so I continued on as usual, using my hands and the stuff I found on the beach to dig holes and build things. Soon, there was one girl beside me helping me dig and before long all three of them had joined.

We worked silently at first but soon were laughing and

shrieking. We pelted each other with sand. We made a tower higher than I ever had alone. I think I was having too much fun that day. Too elated to be in the company of playmates just like me for once to remember the time. Or maybe it was our screams. All I remember is that right at that moment when I realised the sun had gone too far down into the sea and I would need to run off, we saw them. The adults were running toward us screaming and yelling, arms raised over their heads, faces contorted in horror.

We all stood frozen for a moment, before the youngest among us burst into tears at the sight. I didn't know if I should run and abandon my new friends or stay and take a whipping with them. By then, they had surrounded us, each grabbing their own child, shouting at them while yelling at me: "You Witch! Witch child!" I was about to burst into tears when I heard Grandma scream like I had never heard her do before. As she approached, wielding the big stick she kept behind the door of our hut, everyone scattered. That is the one and only time I remember my Grandma beating me. She beat me all the way home.

That night, as I lay curled up trying to fall asleep with my throbbing back and behind, I heard Grandma crying. It was a quiet cry at first, but soon she was wailing and wailing and hitting the floor with her hand. I was still so angry with her for my beating that I was gleeful to hear her crying, but she would not stop until my heart was moved to compassion. I went out and climbed onto her mattress, went under her lappa and laid my hands on her back. At first, she cried even louder, adding rocking to her floor-slapping. Then I became her medicine-woman that night. She talked and talked and talked.

She talked of things I did not understand or remember. She cried that she had not been able to heal my mother in life or in her sickness. She said maybe it was for the best because my mother could not take the taunting over her condition. She cried about what would become of me. How would I marry in a place like this? She hoped that maybe if I learned her trade, I would be ok. People would have no choice but to come to me for medicine like they did to her unless they needed to go to the big city for the big sicknesses. The curse had skipped her too, but what if it fell on me like the townsfolk were waiting to see? She told me she may have to send me away one day if that happened and bade me be strong. She told me never again to disobey her and that maybe now I would understand that being away from her and alone with the townsfolk was dangerous for me. She kept talking until I fell asleep. I woke up the next morning still on her mattress. We got up and went about our day as usual. We never spoke of that day and night again.

After that I kept to myself. I got used to adults whispering around me. They said the same strange things grandma said just loud enough for me to hear. Witch. Curse. They seemed afraid of me, yet they stared at me as if examining me. I learnt to ignore them and went about my chores. I stayed away from the stream and beach for a while but eventually started going back when I could. I didn't stay as long as I used to and if I heard anyone approaching, I ran off home. During this time, I made up an imaginary friend. She became my companion. I talked to her and we played together. At first when I played with her, I worried that if anyone saw me, they would think I was crazy. Then I thought, what did it matter if they added that to the list of words they already said about me?

One day, I told my imaginary friend that I didn't care that people didn't talk or play with me anymore, but I did mind that I could not go to school or the farm. After a while, she seemed to say I should walk to the school and listen from the window. At first, I laughed at her, but when night had come and she had left and I was laying in my bed, I got really really excited about that idea. I started thinking and planning for how I would go, but I knew Grandma wouldn't let me. Then one day, Grandma told me I should go to the market alone. Most of the townsfolk were away anyway because it was harvest and trading time. They had taken canoes across to the other island we could see from ours to supply and trade produce, salt and even fresh water from the springs we have which flowed into my stream in the woods. Some had gone further to the big cities to trade. Also, Grandma said, the market women now knew me well enough to sell to me even if she wasn't with me. So, on trading days I was to go to the market alone and she would get a head start on preparing her remedies. I would later find out that Grandma had a trader friend from inland who passed by on trading days and visited with her while I was at the market.

I left home fleetfooted with excitement and headed straight for the school which was just another five-minute walk from the market. I inched up to the window and peered in. The teacher was writing on a blackboard and I could recognise the marks he was making! They were the same letters I'd been copying from debris on the beach! I watched and listened, learning how to say the sound. I don't know how long I stayed but suddenly a loud bell rang and I saw the children getting up to run outside so I ran as fast as I could to leave the school grounds before they came out. I ran to the market, bought what I needed and then flew home, mouthing the sounds I'd heard all the way home. Grandma didn't seem to mind that I was a little late. She asked why I was so happy and I told her I loved going to market alone. She warned me not to get into any trouble—

"Did the market women give you trouble?" she asked

"No," I said, "they had just asked of you."

I kept going to the school every chance I got, learning through the window. One day, the teacher excused himself in the middle of the lesson and said he was going to the toilet. I stood waiting, sounding in my mind the days of the week which he had been teaching.

M-O-N-D-A-Y.

T-U-E-S-D-A-Y.

W-E-D-N-E-S-D-A-Y.

"Hello. Don't run! I want to talk to you when the kids are at break. Please come wait in my office. Please!"

I had my hand over my mouth to hold back the scream of terror threatening to erupt from my chest. Teacher Musa had gone around so I wouldn't see him approach. I looked at him and decided not to run. I nodded and scurried quickly with him to his office. I didn't want any of the children who knew me to see me and start talking. Teacher Musa left me there and went to finish class.

I sat trembling. Grandma had warned me never to be alone with adults and especially men, but I knew Teacher Musa was a praying man. He was kind and when not at school he was always with the Catholic Mission people—both our own and the white people who seemed to come in and out of our town to teach or talk to the people about their God. Grandma had once told me Teacher Musa had done a good job helping them understand our peoples and our ways because at first, they offended us. I thought I could trust him.

Soon he came back to find me shaking. Before he could talk, I burst into tears and said:

"I just want to come to school! I want to learn! I know letters and sounds and I can write!"

He looked at me, part astonished, part amused.

"I know" he said.

He handed me a blank paper and pencil. It was the first time I had held a pencil.

"Write me some letters." I wrote:

F-A-N-T-A

M-O-N-D-A-Y

T-U-E-S-D-A-Y

He said: "who taught you how to write?"

I said, "myself."

Teacher Musa said: "Okay, I need to come talk to your Grandma."

I told him I was scared. She would be mad and she would never let me come.

He said: "Leave it with me. God will make a way."

Teacher Musa didn't come for a week. By the time he came, I was a nervous wreck. Grandma told him to come later. She did not see people so early in the afternoon. He pleaded with her and said he didn't want to talk when the townsfolk were around because he wanted to talk to her about helping me. That got her attention and we all went inside to sit and talk. Teacher Musa told Grandma he would personally supervise me and that he had arranged with the missionaries to give me all the school supplies I needed for the rest of that school year. He told Grandma I was too smart not to be allowed to go to school. Grandma listened, expressionless as he droned on and on. I rocked back and forth. My heart felt like stone. She would never say yes.

"Yes."

"She can go. But you must swear with your life that you will take care of her. She must learn because I fear she will get the mark and carry the curse. You must protect her so she can learn and leave this place. I thank you and the missionaries for the supplies, but next year I will pay."

I jumped up and started dancing! "I am going to school! I am going to learn!" I hugged and kissed grandma. I twirled. I had never been so happy. That evening, my imaginary friend and I danced on the beach.

School was the best days of my life. I discovered that I was not only quick to pick up English but also numbers and math. I loved it so much that I didn't even notice or care the first few days when kids ignored me and a couple of boys called me names and threatened to stone me. Teacher Musa dealt with them right away and sent them to the Principal's office. By the end of the first month, the kids were civil to me even though they didn't play with me on the playground. By the end of the term, it was clear I was almost top of the class. My classmates still did not play with me, but they were almost kind. By the end of the school year, I was helping my classmates with homework. I felt like Grandma. I knew they didn't like me, but they engaged with me because they needed my help. And they respected me for my mind.

Grandma started doing house calls as well as going with the traders to the other island and even the mainland to share her remedies so she could make money. She wasn't afraid of leaving me because I was so busy studying, I didn't leave the hut as much when she was away. I would read and read and practice and practice until it was too dim in the hut to study. One day, Grandma came back with a solar-powered light and I was overjoyed. I stayed up late into the night studying from then on. I continued to love school and thrive throughout Primary School. By then, I had learned that my island, the place I called home, was Tasso Island on the Sierra Leone River Estuary, off the coast of Freetown.

Teacher Musa continued to support and guide me when I left primary school. Then at the end of primary, I had to go over to Lokomasama Chiefdom to Secondary School, further inland. To make it easy for me, I stayed there with the nuns. It was hard for me to leave Grandma, but by then I was learning so much, I knew that being away for school was for the best. I visited Grandma and helped her as usual every weekend. I would then walk on the beach, sharing everything I was learning with my imaginary friend

It was during this time that Grandma's greatest fears came to pass. One day as I showered, Grandma asked to come into our shower house to get the underclothes she'd left hanging on the line we had strung there for that purpose. The shower house was a tall and narrow concrete structure with a window up high for light. I'm told my Pa built it to make sure we had privacy. It was tucked in the corner of our yard where there was no passage or access to the woods. I always felt secure in there. It was the only time I felt connected to the father I had never seen. I unlatched the door for Grandma and turned to return to my bucket and washing. I heard a gasp and spun around to find Grandma leaning on the door frame, hands on her head which was rocking side to side as if a screw in her neck had suddenly loosened. She kept drawing in deep breaths and exhaling the sound "Ah! Ah! Ah! Ah!"

I rushed to her and held the sides of her face to keep her head steady.

"Mama! Mama! Wetin apin" *Mama. What's happening?*

My heart was racing. Was she ill? Getting a heart attack? She hadn't even looked this shocked or dazed when I had my first monthly period. She held my wet soapy shoulders, managed to tell me to finish off and meet her inside and rushed out, a trail of *Ahs* following her.

I quickly finished and rushed inside. Grandma had collected herself somewhat. I sat on a bench facing her as she explained. The marks my mother had all over her face and hands had started appearing on my back. It was the mark that had changed the colour of my mother's eyes and made it swell sometimes and affected inside her mouth too. The townsfolk said it was a curse and a bad omen and that the family had been bewitched in long times past. Many in our line seem to have it and the ones who have it never last. They have a mishap fall upon them or develop other witching powers the story goes. When my father said he would marry and take care of my mother, the townsfolk said he'd been bewitched.

I listened silently, then asked Grandma what she thought. She was quiet for a minute. She said she thought it was an illness, but she couldn't understand or seem to cure it no matter what she tried. She said it was true that those who had it did not last or seem to court death. In her own lifetime, she said, her mother had got it and was constantly ill until she died. Another cousin who had got it became deaf and ran mad before he died. I told Grandma not to worry. I would learn what this sickness was now that I went to school and I would not die of it. This seemed to reassure her, but she bade me cover my marks. The townsfolk had begun to accept me. She didn't want me to have to pull from school if they got agitated or concerned. I told her the nuns would not let that happen.

When I went back to school, I showed the nuns my marks. They were on the left side of my back underneath my armpits. Sister Margaret explained to me that it was a condition called Vitiligo. Teacher Musa came with the laptop and we researched it. I learned that exposure to the sun makes it spread faster, so with Grandma's admonition and this knowledge, I stopped wearing tank tops. The nuns and Teacher Musa prayed with me and promised to help me. They told me not to worry. The nuns watched with me as we monitored the progress of the marks. They snaked down my back almost to my hips. The marks eventually travelled through my armpit and down my left upper arm. At that point there was no hiding the contrast between my dark chocolate skin and the marks, so I started wearing long-sleeved shirts only. This started rumours in both my town and the school area. One day, I woke up and decided I was tired of hiding. I went to school in a tee-shirt. The map drawn by the vitiligo ran down my arm as clear as day and night.

At first, the clock seemed to rewind and I was back at my first day in primary school when no one would speak to me or play with me. Everyone stared and whispered but I was used to that so I just carried on as usual. After lunch, the Principal and one of the nuns came in to talk to the class. They explained what my skin condition was and said they expected people to treat me as they would want to be treated in my circumstance. They asked if anyone had any questions.

"Is it contagious? My mom said it is and that's why …"

The Principal explained that I was not, in fact, contagious. That it was mostly hereditary. This created both a collective sigh and a buzz in the class as some expressed relief while others proceeded to explain what their parents had told them about the contagion of the disease. The Principal held up his hand and asked whether I wanted to say anything. I said simply:

"Thank you for your kindness in explaining. Of course, I would like not to be ostracised, but because of this condition in my family I am used to people being concerned and will be fine whether people choose to play with me or not. As for the question of contagion, I just wish to let people know my Grandmother has lived with me and my mother before me who had it and she has not a single spot. In the weeks after that, my classmates slowly thawed and we were soon back to normal. I continued to be thankful the tracks didn't spread to my face.

When I had a year left for secondary school, Teacher Musa asked to take me on the ferry to Freetown, where we visited the British Council. There was an opportunity for me to take the exam called SAT that might help me get a scholarship and there was a preparation session there. I went through the practice books they had on the first day we were there. I loved the math but noticed that some of the topics they asked to write about in the essay section made no sense to me and I didn't know the names of the famous people they talked about. I decided to use my imagination as best as I could. I stayed up all night that day researching and reading about some of the topics I had encountered – drones, quantum physics, space engineering. I was fascinated. The next day I took the practice test and Teacher Musa was ecstatic! He could not stop talking all the way back on the ferry from Freetown to Lungi and on the 30-minute drive to Lokomasama. He said I aced the test and if I did that well in the real one next year, I could go on to any top university I wanted. Indeed, that is how I found myself at the airport one evening, saying goodbye to Grandma, Teacher Musa and Grandma's friend Pa Modu who I had finally met. Grandma's eyes were red but they also reflected a deep peace.

"You are free now my granddaughter. Study well." She said as she bade me farewell.

I was en route to Columbia Engineering.

My success in passing the SATs and gaining such a successful college outcome and full scholarship had resulted in an unexpected surprise. When the news spread, the market women who had seen me growing up with Grandma sent a delegation to our home. They all chip in monthly to collect a pot of money—called *osusu*, they said, which was given every month to one of the women in the *osusu* circle to expand her business. They had decided to give me that month's pot of money instead to help support my travels. Next came families and groups of Grandma's clients. They brought food, gifts, clothing and money. Those who were still suspicious of us left their offerings at the door and silently left. But on the day I was leaving, we emerged from the hut to find the womenfolk in our backyard kitchen, cooking for us. Some of them were the mothers who had screamed in fear at me on the beach when I played with their kids in childhood. Some were those children, now carrying their own babies in wraps on their backs.

They helped us pack. They prayed with us when Grandma called the Imam to do a farewell prayer. Then as I took my bags to leave for the airport via a stop to say goodbye to the teachers, Principals and nuns at Lokomasama, they burst out in song. It was a celebration of their daughter who they described as a genie—one given the gift of genius that came with her marks. I laughed and cried at the irony of it all, even as the joy of being called their own warmed my heart in ways I had never experienced.

~~~

I loved New York City. I found it fascinating that a place so different from my home felt so familiar. It might have been the fact that on any given day I might meet a fellow Sierra Leonean at the subway or on the shops along 125th or on my brisk walk to Fu Foundation School of Engineering. Or that despite its ultimate cosmopolitan feel and city skyline, trash piles collected on the streets to remind us that humans occupied the concrete jungle. It may even be that in the hub of Times Square which seemed to have more people than I ever saw on my island in one day, I was anonymous and no one stared at me or whispered. I can't decide, but I loved it and felt at home. I loved that I could buy African black soap and raw shea butter, the exact kind the women at the Tasso Island market sold, in the African store next to the Ghanaian Episcopalian church. I loved that I could buy cassava leaves and hot peppers and pretend I am walking home to my hut and to Grandma.

I loved walking briskly along. I loved watching the neighbourhoods change as the peoples of the world congregated there placed their mark on each of their blocks. I loved the buzz of diverse languages, yet the unique twang of every New Yorker. I loved her skyline, because lady liberty gave me hope. But the Tree of Hope did that even more when I touched it, imaging all those before me who had. I wondered what their hopes and prayers were. And on a
~~~

daily basis, I saw that hope in all the peoples of every continent I met at Columbia and on the New York streets. The countries and seasons I had read about in geography came alive in New York City. I loved that. I loved sitting and reading in Central Park. And most of all I loved that the streets were named after the African American Greats of the Black Liberation struggles. In all the hustle and bustle, walking along Frederick Douglass Boulevard or Martin Luther King Boulevard or Malcolm X Boulevard made Harlem feel like hallowed ground for me. It made me feel like home to walk the spaces named after the ancestors that had been brought by force and yet who didn't let oppression dampen their greatness.

In New York, I got some medical care for my vitiligo that the nuns had arranged for me. I learned that I had the segmental kind that was quite localised and seemed to have stopped, although they cautioned there was a chance it could start spreading again. They gave me tips about avoiding sunburn and keeping stress down so as not to trigger further spreads. They offered camouflage creams and creams that could help restore pigmentation. Since it wasn't affecting my appearance, treatments such as skin grafts and pigmentation processes were not recommended and would be too expensive anyway. As I left the doctors' offices, I realised I felt very much at peace. I never used the creams.

When I first arrived, I worried about the cold in autumn and winter and how I would adjust to the seasons. What I grew to love was the fact that I didn't have to work hard to keep my marks covered most of the year. In the summer, I perfected looks that paired wide-brimmed summer hats with sheer silk scarfs to mostly cover my left arm from sun exposure when I wore tank tops and short-sleeved shirts. It was wearing this look when an agent stopped me on the streets of Manhattan one day and asked if I would do a portfolio photoshoot and sign up to do modelling gigs. I saw no reason not to, so I did the shoot. It was an uncanny experience—both unsettling and affirming. I had never been so admired before for my height, cheekbones, almond eyes, and even my vitiligo. I went on to do photo advertisements for everything from makeup to clothing in the years to follow. More often than not, my vitiligo was the star of the shoot.

The days flew by fast. My life was focused on the endless hours of studying engineering and modelling. I woke up one day almost in my third year realizing that I had many acquaintances but no strong friendships. A dull sense of loneliness settled over me. I started feeling homesick even though I spoke to Grandma regularly via WhatsApp which she knew how to use better than I did. I was also one of two female students in my class and while Helen Li was friendly, we had both been pretty distant, not quite connecting beyond our shared studies. In desperation, I started speaking to my imaginary friend to fill the void in my apartment. That was when I realised I needed to find community to keep from losing my mind. I started looking for more active ways to meet other African immigrants and Black students. I found myself at the Black History Month panel talk, featuring a speaker by the name of Dr Haja Ajara Johnson, A History and Africana studies visiting professor from Harvard.

Dr Johnson as I had suspected was from Sierra Leone. I enjoyed hers and the panels responses to questions about race relations in America, but it was her closing remarks that changed my life. She spoke of the history of Sierra Leone as both a slave trading British outpost and a receiver of repatriated freed slaves from Nova Scotia, Britain and recaptives from slave ships after slave trade became illegal. She was a descendant of those groups. Her ancestry was of the Igbo captives who settled in Murray town and formed part of the communities of Fourah Bay that continue to-date. I was spellbound on the edge of my chair. How had I not been taught this history? How did I not know this about my own country? As my brain whirled, I heard her say Bunce Island and I edged even further on my seat, transfixed. Bunce Island was the island across from my home island! It was the place the traders went to monthly and where Grandma had started going to do house calls to supplement her income and support me through school. I had never been there.

Heat rose to my head and it felt constricted as Dr Johnson explained the role of King James and King George in establishing the Royal African Company to operate a slave fort out of Bunce Island. Operating out of Bunce Island since 1670!! She described the subsequent situations—agreements and payments to local chiefs to operate and trade, the change to privately owned companies of Grant Oswald and company followed by the John & Alexander Anderson company. The tens of thousands of slaves shipped from Bunce Island, first to the Caribbean and then as preferred cargo to Georgia and South Carolina for their rice planting skills. The constant raids by the Dutch, Luso-Portugese, then the French! She talked of the strategic role of the Freetown colony in the abolition movement and the conflicting role it played as a haven for freed slaves, even while others were being shipped off her beautiful beach island shores. Dr Johnson spoke of the difficulties of the initial settlers and settlement —clashes with the locals as well as the British leaders sent to administer the colony, the challenges of the weather and the dissonance of knowing the trade continued even as they lived free.

The air felt suffocating around me. I felt the collective heaviness of the black brethren gathered, African and Caribbean immigrants and African-Americans, taking in all that this meant for our ancestors before us and for us present. I also felt a heaviness of heart for what I had not known right at my doorstep and was just hearing in New York City, oceans and worlds away from the scenes being described. A group of us had dinner afterwards. There was anger. There was pain. There was sorrow. There were radical entreaties by those who bade us stay 'woke.' There was guilt and relief by those who were grateful for being born in these times. There was talk about whether these times were much better. Hell, any of us could get shot on the way home. We drank a bit too much. Overall, we left with a sense of bonding and unity. And I left with numbers for Shane, Imani and Dawna and a date for dinner at Sylvia's the next week.

I became obsessed with Sierra Leone's role in the slave trade history. I researched Bunce Island. I read Yema Lucinda Hunter books, *Road to Freedom* and *Her name was Aina.* I looked up the story of the Black Loyalists and read and watched the documentary *Rough Crossings: Britain, the Slaves and the American Revolution.* I did not go a day without ruminating on the stories and the connections. When I was not studying, I was reading about Sierra Leone's role in the saga of the transatlantic slave trade history. I made up my mind I had to go home after graduation. I needed to see Grandma and I needed to visit Bunce Island and see the relics of the slave fort there for myself. It was a whole year before I left for that homeward journey, but that year is a blur.

When I arrived back in Sierra Leone and walked on the shores of Tasso Island, I felt like I was in a time capsule. I could not stop thinking about what it would have been like and felt like for those taken or for those who returned. I began to hear their cries in the winds. I was impatient to go to Bunce Island but Grandma would have none of it. She wanted me to meet and greet those who had continued to be helpful to her since I left. I decided to rest easy and give it a few days before going to Bunce.

Grandma looked hale and hearty, though tell-tale signs of aging showed in her slightly slower pace and drooping shoulders. There were lines around her eyes that were not there when I left, but it was the new peace in the depth of her eyes that most enlivened me. She and Pa Modu still saw each other regularly and she had found community in the market women, some of whom she was now teaching her knowledge of herbs and healing roots. She had so many questions and I had so much to tell her! I waited for the right moment for us to speak. During that time, I was walking back from the market carrying gifts from one of the women when I heard a mischief-laced voice say: "Well hello, Mi Padi!" Chills of excitement ran up my spine. The accent was different but the voice unmistakable. It was Hassan. He was in town from England where he was studying.

Hassan and I chatted incessantly as if to catch up on everything from the day we were forbidden from speaking because of our misdemeanour. We reminisced about it, laughing ourselves to tears. It was so easy to be with him. We took the walk down memory lane to the stream, talking about what our lives were like now. At the stream, I told him about my vitiligo and we found ourselves undressing without words. He examined my vitiligo and kissed it. We examined ourselves as we had when we were children and the inevitable started happening as our adult bodies responded to our hands on each other. As he moved to enter me, he realised I was a virgin. He stopped, looking at me inquiringly, a shocked look in his eyes. I smiled and nodded my consent. He whispered into my lips:

"How come? Are you sure?"

I said: "I haven't had time for romance and haven't been interested in the quick sex version that seems enough for my friends."

He said: "And this isn't casual?"

I said: "Maybe it is, but it feels right."

Afterwards, we lay in the grass, talking and relishing the moment as long as we could. When it was time to go, we exchanged numbers as he said: "may I call you when we go back?" I said: "I'd like that, but only if you want to." We walked back holding hands. We kissed as we parted ways. He was off to Freetown the next day.

Grandma and I finally had a quiet moment a couple days later for our talk. Grandma listened patiently as I poured out about my time away and about what I had learned about Bunce Island and why

I wanted to go see the fort as soon as possible. My words spilled over each other as I couldn't get them out fast enough it seemed and I worried that she would tire of my diatribe. That night, I experienced why the townsfolks had visited Grandma every night with their problems. She was unflinching as she took it all in. When I was complete and out of breath, she finally spoke:

"It is true what you heard. Our people know about this and I pass the old fort every time I go with the traders. Others like you who have now gone across the seas and even the ancestors of the White Folk who traded our people come regularly to look at it. Djeli Musu's son, Ibrahim, he is their narrative and interpreter. He explains some of the stories of old to them. You will go tomorrow. He will show you and explain to you, but first you must go see Djeli Musu in the morning. I had left instructions to her that should I die before you return, she should tell you the story of our family. There is more you need to know. I am alive, but it was Djeli Musu who explained it all to me so I will have her explain to you. I will come but she will tell you the story. It will help you understand what you did not before." Grandma said no more, no matter how much I pleaded. I barely slept a wink that night, sweating both from the 35-degree heat and my pounding anxious heart.

Djeli Musu barely had any teeth left. She was bent over with age but it was clear she had once been a striking beauty. She spoke only Themne and I was thankful I still understood although I was rusty in my speech. I knew enough to greet her, offering kola nut to show I came in peace and gave her rice, spices and produce from the market. She thanked me profusely and took a bite of kolanut to signify she had accepted my offering. I could not tell how she managed to bite and chew on the kolanut while being toothless. She asked Grandma if it was time to tell the story again. When Grandma nodded, she folded the half chewed kolanut in the top folds of her wrapper, took out a pack of the local tobacco called snuff and launched in, putting a pinch of snuff in her mouth occasionally throughout the telling.

An hour later, I was holding Grandma's hand, tears silently streaming down my face, creating marks like my vitiligo tracks. I had just learned that my Grandmother's Great-Grandmother was a beautiful woman, a relative of Djeli Musu's ancestral line. From childhood, she had been betrothed to Chief Or Bai's son. She proved to be as intelligent as she was beautiful. Quick minded and quick tongued. It is said the Chief's advisors told him she should not become his daughter-in-law but it was too late. His son was smitten and they married as soon as her womanhood blood appeared and she completed her rites of passage. The new bride began to question matters that only men did. In those days, the slave trading fort was on our beloved Tasso Island, not on the place now called Bunce Island. She asked: Why did we encourage the white man to use our lands? Why were people being sold to them like sheep? Was it not clear how brutally they were being treated? If they are treated so now, how will they be treated in the lands they were traded to? It is said everyone bade her stop, but when she could take it no more, she did a great misdeed. She began to sneak out at night and unchain the ones captured and held in the court, awaiting sale when the white man came on trading days.

After several groups of captives escaped, the court became suspicious. The escapees were causing them to lose money and the white men who came to trade were getting angry that there was not enough cargo. They set a trap. The trap caught the young woman. She was tied overnight and brought to the palaver hut for questioning and sentencing the next day. The men decided she would be given to the white men along with the next group of captives to be sold. It is said her husband tried to save her, but he had just completed his manhood rites and did not want to appear weak. When it became clear his father and the court would not relent, he stood back and let his bride be sold, leaving behind a three-year-old daughter. It is said she cursed them even as she was being dragged away.

After that, Chief Or Bai gave his son to the traders to help them build another fort on Bunce Island. It was smaller, escape would be much harder and giving his son to work with the traders was a peace offering, a sign of good will. It became the main trading post and our island was turned into a plantation and supply base. His son became as the white man. He dressed like them, he drank from their flasks, he even took on their name and became known as Henry Adams. I was told his grave resided at Bunce Island and Ibrahim would show it to me.

"What became of the little girl," I asked. She was constantly ill. She managed to marry and have a son, but then passed away when he was a few years old. Her son became stricken with the mark around the same time his mother died, so the people said it was the curse of his grandmother. They said she used witchcraft to kill her daughter from across the seas so she would not be enslaved. Then, they said, she ensured all her offspring were marked so they would also not be good to sell to the white man. Over the years, the legend thickened whenever those of her line or with the marks became ill. The townsfolk began to think being around them would bring the same bad luck.

I collected myself and went with Ibrahim in one of the fishing canoes across to Bunce Island. Ibrahim walked me through it all. The pier where my Grandmother's Great-Grandmother walked to her fate. The canons still engraved with King George's emblem, the spaces where male and female captives were held, the fireplace where they were branded, the dungeon where they were kept for some days before going through the door of no return, and then the grave of Henry Adams. It was there I broke down. Cursing, crying, stomping and beating his grave until my hands were bruised and my tears spent. I felt little life left in me as Ibrahim rowed me back to Tasso Island afterwards.

The rest of the holiday was a daze. I put a brave face on for Grandma but instead I felt like something in me died. Although it was freeing to understand the isolation and ostracization of my childhood, I felt burdened with the pain and unfairness that all my ancestors had suffered. I visited the Secondary School in Lokomasama and visited with the nuns and that helped. I spent time with Teacher Musa and his family. He had married and they already had two sons. We talked long into the night and he encouraged me as he had always done. He told me God had saved me and revealed these things to me for a reason. I could not see the reason. I was spent.

I returned to New York a zombie. I managed to feed myself and go to my modelling gigs but other than that it was as if time had frozen for me at Henry Adams grave. Whether asleep or awake I saw the imagined images of my maternal ancestor. I saw her trying to speak up and being shut down. I imagined what she thought when she decided to set the captives free. I felt the bravery and fear in her soul when she was caught in the act and the betrayal and terror of being handed over to the slavers. I saw her stepping off the pier to be rowed to the waiting ship. She, a Chief's wife, stowed away with all the others. Slavery was no respecter of persons. These images played in my mind until I thought I'd gone mad.

One morning I noticed my vitiligo had spread. It had laced around my left arm and up to my neck. That's when I realised I had to stop the madness. I decided to busy my body and mind to save myself. I started taking exercise classes at the ladies' gym around the corner—everything from yoga to spin classes to belly dancing. I registered for piano lessons. I decided I would take another month or two to get my head straight before following-up on leads for work in engineering. I had some open offers from places where I had interned.

One day, I did a modelling gig at the public library on Harry Belafonte and 115th. Afterwards, I meant to run out to belly dancing class. Instead, on the way out, I found myself sitting at a computer staring at the search field of the online catalogue. Then I placed my fingers on the keyboard and watched the letters appearing on my screen. *Sierra Leone.* Two hours later, I was sitting on the floor with books scattered around me in the *Sc* section, cataloguing all things African history. I had everything on the floor beside me from *Slavery, abolition and the transition to colonialism in Sierra Leone to slave logbooks* to *Encyclopedia of African History* to *Slavery and Slaving in African History* and the one I was engrossed in—*Narrative of Two Voyages to the River Sierra Leone during the Years 1791-1792-1793* edited and annotated by Christopher Fyfe. There was also a pile of dirty tissues beside me from the tissue box I'd co-opted from the toilet. As I read through Narratives of Two Journeys, Anna Maria Falconbridge's letters told the background story of Bunce and Tasso Island that Djeli Musu had told me. My head started throbbing. I decided to check-out the book and leave. As I packed up, I discovered the whole section of slave narratives and biographies. I added the *Classic Slave Narratives* to my check-out pile.

For the next three months I shuttled back and forth to the library every chance I got. I told myself to stop but the knowledge I was gaining was cathartic and behind the pain a strange relief started taking place. I recognised that I had journeyed through shock and denial, but now healing and acceptance were taking over. And I was grateful, so grateful to be standing on the shoulders of all I read and learned about. Slave Narratives, often subtitled written by herself/himself were my favourite. I started looking beyond the books to the original texts and less popular stories housed in black-authored anti-slavery newsletters like the *Liberator* during the abolition era. I was spellbound by them.

I could not fathom the bravery of these men, women and children who chose agency and freedom in the midst of impossible human evil, degradation and suffering. My heart bled for the injustices they had experienced but as it bled, I became convinced that the world needed more love and healing and I got stronger every day. I began to be able to look at the white person across from me on the subway without thinking and seeing slaver. I knew my reading and learning would continue, but I finally felt strong enough to get on with life. A strong desire to work for social justice was building in my soul.

One day, I stopped by the library again on my way from one of three interviews I had lined up. I was going through slave narratives in one of the anti-slavery columns when my eyes fell on a title. *Me stayed Royal and Free – The story of Fatima Musu Sama, as written by herself.* I blinked and read and reread the title. My brain refused to process what it was reading and my heart felt like it would burst from my chest.

> *Me stayed free. No matter the beatings. No matter how much me massa force imsef on me. No matter how me mistress peel me skin wit de whip, me remember, me name not Sarah Boyki as dem call me. I never forget me name. Me tell mesef everyday me name Fatima Musu Sama. I never forget me beautiful even wit beat mark 'pon me face. Me helped me people get free. Me know I get free one day. God bless General Tubman, she Moses true! She help me journey to freedom lek me hep orda people before. Ah freedom so sweet! It refresh me soul like dem coconut juice 'pon de fruit of the trees in me land befo dem try to destroy me. But now, my fellow free blacks dem talking of going back der. Me art say no. Me family dem sell me one time, Chief Or Bai fit sell me again if I return. Last ship lef already for 'Frica but me no go. Me pray dem safe en not back in de slave ship's belly every day. No, me like me freedom en me like helping orda people know this business evil. Me art also scare all de black folk disappearing en take back south. Back to de life after dem find free! No, if me slave again, me kill mesef. Me head tell me to go follow de railroad further Nort wit dem people going to de place call Canada. Me know slaves der too but me herr free colony there also. Me decide me go wit Mr. Henson. We get herr safe. We fine and we stay free.*

It was dated 1830, but published a hundred years later in a series about the Dawn Settlement in Dresden, Upper Canada.

That is how I found myself at the offices of one Samuel Sam, Counselling Psychologist practising in Toronto, Ontario. Tracing Fatima's journey led me to him. I had made an appointment as a potential client. He walked out to meet me in the consulting room where the legal assistant had directed me to wait. The room was warm, adorned with earthy tones and tranquil nature images. I sat, clenching and unclenching my hands in my lap. I was armed with the copies of records and document clippings that seemed to be on fire in my lap. Sweat beads adorned my forehead in spite of the sub-20-degrees weather. Samuel walked out to greet me and stretched out his hand to grasp mine in a warm handshake. There were unmistakable vitiligo tracks snaking out from under his shirt cuff onto his hand.

"Hey! I know you" he exclaimed "You're the model in the ads at the malls! Thanks for representing. Vitiligo runs in my family too."

I laughed as tears leapt to my eyes. "I know you know me and I know vitiligo runs in your family…"

Two years later, when Hassan and I got married in New York, Samuel's family and all the others we had traced from St Kitts, Georgia, Charleston, New York and Ontario were in the pews. Some had vitiligo, others didn't. It was Samuel who walked me down the aisle. Then the Pastor asked:

"Who gives this woman to be married to this man?"

Grandma and Teacher Musa, standing on either side of me at the foot of the alter, answered in unison.

"We do!"

5. THE ANCESTORS

The horn blaring in her face shook Ana from her blackout. As consciousness dawned through the fog of her mind, she realised the side of her face was stuck to the steering wheel from her own drool. She laughed out loud uncontrollably, unglued her face and sat up to stop the blaring. She looked out the window to get her bearings and was greeted by the toothless smile and piercing eyes of her ninety-year old neighbour who never seemed to sleep and was certainly all-knowing. Ana tried not to yelp.

She was secretly scared of Mrs. Owen who she called Mrs. O, because she had replaced Owen for Owl a long time ago. She gulped some air to compose herself before rolling down the window:

"Good evening Mrs. O"

"Good evening darlin.' Just walked over to check on you. Strange seeing you sitting in yo' carport with yo' head down for 15 minutes dear. No man or that girlfriend of yours wit the multicoloured cropped hair in the front seat wit you eida. You ok, love."

"Yes, Mrs. O. I'm ok. Just a bit tired from a few long days—that's all"

"Ok—you take care now. Can't be working yourself into a stupor just coz you don't have any family of yo own to worry about. How're you gonna get a date if you always working?"

Ana smiled and rolled up her window to signal she wasn't going to go there. She grabbed her coffee mug and took a gulp of the long-cold, somewhat stale brew. She was suddenly aware of hunger pangs coursing through her as her stomach growled. Still laughing out loud, she reached for her phone, turned on the camera and took a selfie. She hit share and sent it off to Adama in a WhatsApp message:

Just woke up red-eyed and drooling on my steering wheel…in the carport. The struggle is real! BTW—The Owl came to check on me right as I woke up because I wasn't moving and "she didn't see no man or my friend wit the multi-coloured crop in my front seat." Argh and shivers!!

Typing….

Ouch! Low blow from Mrs. O! But you do look rough! Friend with the multicoloured crop—LOL! She still can't say my name?

Yep. You are still A-dam which she knows is wrong or Adamu, which I've told her is a different African name, so you are just my friend wit the multi-coloured crop. Adama really shouldn't be that hard…

Typing….

Oh, about that—I changed my colour to blue today

LOL!!! For real? You're a mess!

Typing….

ok—get your butt inside and get some nourishment and rest. No fancy shakes either—get you some of the jollof rice and chicken I brought over on the weekend coz I know it's still in your fridge

Typing….

You haven't called Brian yet have you?

Nope

Typing….

You should call him…but you know that already. Go eat. Ttyl.

The weight of the decisions facing her came crashing down—shoulders slumping under the weight. Her stomach was suddenly queasy. Her hunger fled. She collected herself and her laptop bag and finally got out of the car. She walked in and threw the keys on her lobby table, set her laptop bag down and headed to the kitchen. She opened the fridge. The block of cheddar cheese had gone moldy so she threw it out. Adama's jollof rice and chicken stared at her. She stared blankly back.

Brian, my answer is yes.

She mindlessly took out the food to start serving. She served some rice which smelt amazing. She opened the stew bowl. There was too much oil floating on top. She stirred to the bottom and started examining the meat and chicken. The chicken did not look like the organic farm chicken she preferred at all, even though Adama told her it was. *Lying through her teeth as usual just to get me to eat the crap she cooks.*

Brian, my answer is no.

Her forehead developed dew from the moisture that instantly oozed from her body. She felt like gaging even though her stomach shouldn't have enough food to give up. She went to the bathroom and retched a bit into the sink. She could taste bile at the back of her throat but nothing came out. Serious decisions had always made her sick.

Phillip, I need to talk to you.

She reached for the sink to steady herself as she felt the room spin a bit. Clearly, she needed food. Thinking about it all on an empty stomach was making her nerves worse. She went back to the kitchen and pulled out her pre-packaged servings of Kale, fruit blends, yogurts and protein mix from *Healthy Eats, Healthy life*. She didn't know how she'd survive without that store. Last time she was there the nutritionist speaker they had on was amazing and had totally sold her on cutting processed foods from her diet. She poured the assortment into her shake mug, popped it into the blender, hit start and watched it spin. When it reached the right consistency of mash, she stopped the blender and took a gulp. She instantly felt the tingling relief of nourishment coursing through her starved body. She closed her eyes, enjoying the feeling as she took another swig from her shake mug. She felt steadier now. When she opened her eyes, they fell on the letter on the kitchen counter.

Dear Ms. Kay…please confirm by September 15…

Ana leaned forward and rested her head on the kitchen cabinet above her. She felt weary as confusion washed over her again. How was she to decide? If her lawyer colleagues who always thought she had it together could see her now.

Her eyes drifted to the world clock across the open concept divider wall between the kitchen and dining room that she only used when her parents visited. The world clock on the dining room wall said it was September 14, but in GMT it was already 4:00 a.m., which meant it was September 15 elsewhere in the world, including most of West Africa—and Sierra Leone.

She smiled thinking of the last time her parents came to visit from Sierra Leone. Their visit had coincided with her baby sister Maria's and her perfect family from London. Her parents in their usual nomadic style had flown to New Castle and spent a month with Maria and her husband Sam, en route to visit her for another month. Sam was a surgeon by day and also an Elder and lay pastor at the Anglican church they attended. His occupations were the only reason her parents had forgiven Maria for marrying an English boy, in pure English style—with no traditional ceremonies in England or back in Sierra Leone.

Even now, Ana had to listen to her mother retelling the story regularly, as if the retelling will imbue in Ana's mind that she is not to repeat the offenses.

> "Imagine!! This Maria stood on London Bridge and accepted a ring from Sam. Then she had the guts to send us the video on WhatsApp with the message: Guess what happened today!!!! Ah!! Your dad and I played the video in disbelief. There she was on London bridge with Kumi and Sara and Mohammed—all there in the group cheering while Sam knelt to give her a ring! Couldn't they have advised her to call us first! They should at least know the culture and how much that would offend your dad! A-ah!! Then she had the nerve to tell us ***they*** had decided on a small garden wedding and ***we*** were invited! Invited! Do they think they are the Royals! They should have known better!"

That last visit was no different. Any time Maria was out at the park or shopping with Sam and their beyond adorable kids Ali and baby Ana, Ana got to hear Mom's complaints about their non-traditional ways, followed by the small mercies she approved of:

> "Thank God Sam is serving in the church! Your sister is serving now too. She is coordinating the children's ministry. You should talk to her about how she's managing to serve even with work and family. You can't be too busy for God, my dear."

Ana would politely smile—she was used to the subliminal and overt messages directed at her and her life. She didn't take it personally.

She and Maria were too close to care about all the ways they could have been pitted against each other if they took Mom's comparisons too seriously. They had sorted out their roles early in life. Maria had always been the carefree one who did whatever she wanted without arguing with Mama. Ana tried to please as much as she could but at some point, had let go of being perfect elder child. She could never be the firstborn son Mama never had…and she had accepted that growing up in England, going to school in Canada and now working and living in America meant she would always be a strange flower to her Sierra Leonean family.

Funnily, after registering his displeasure that Maria was insisting on no 'traditional fanfare,' Dad had been silent about it. It was difficult to tell whether his silence was resignation or approval but Ana had noticed an overall softening in him in those days, as if age had rounded his edges along with the gait of his shoulders. He still stood and spoke like the Judge in him that she had always admired. He still made edicts and drew quick conclusions on everything from the news to what puppy she should buy—she had always admired the clarity and quickness of his mind. But she had noticed he no longer insisted on his way or the highway. He issued his judgements more like shards of wisdom to pick from even when he had a clear preference. He had laid down his gavel.

She recalled Mom's voice now, in her final plea as they loaded their bags into Maria's rental to start their homeward journey:

"Ana, my dear—please consider getting married. You can't tell me there is still no one who interests you…you are doing so well and we are proud…but how can you live in this big empty house alone? Or have you become too feminist to consider marriage?"

Maria had come in for a hug right then—their flight was later but they planned to go see Mom and Dad safely checked-in, and then would take their time to return the rental, get through security with the kids and have lunch calmly while they waited for their flights inside the gates.

"Don't roll your eyes" she whispered with a twinkle in her eyes—"just tell her you're planning to start living with Brian next month so you won't be alone. Or that Adama is more than your girlfriend—let's see how she takes that!"

They collapsed into each other in peals of laughter.

"I don't care what you two are laughing about! I'm your mother. It's my duty to tell you what's right. Ah! We have lost you to western ways!"

Maria had blown Mom a kiss and sailed out to adjust the car seats. Ana still remembers that last hug she gave Mom—with an extra squeeze while she still chuckled. She remembers Dad touching her cheek. It was strange because his show of affection had always been to pat her on the head. He'd said "be well, daughter." She had instinctively put her hand over his, as if to catch and hold the sensation before he broke away. Now, she raised her hand back to her face to recall the moment; and with that came the racking sobs of her grief. Two months after her parents last visit, Adama had arrived for a visit, unannounced. Ana found out later that Adama had sent Aunty Madinatu a WhatsApp message from the car so Aunty would know she was there before she called. *The news isn't good my child. They were going to a wedding in Bo…hit by a lorry…3 cars in the accident…Your Papa died on the spot. Your Mama was struggling at first but she's gone too, my child. They are gone…*

Her grief had not dulled over the 5 years since…and on days like today, she longed for a shard of wisdom from Dad. She would even take his gavel or Mom's nagging. She realised now how much their ways had guided her even when they were annoying. Oh, how she longed for that today! She cried herself ugly.

~~~

The town crier flew around calling the gathering.

Fambul dem! Assanatu Kargbo im Fambul dem. Tem don reach for geda. Tem don reach for geda. Make we geda, fambul dem.

Family and relatives of Assanatu Kargbo—it's time to gather. It's time to gather.

Watta the Wise groaned. She unfolded herself from the corner she prefers to occupy these days. She had the perfect view of eternity from there. Diamond-shaped, beautiful—a cacophony of shades and hues and angles. She spends her time studying each opening or gateway until the colours erupt and contort and the
~~~

clearing happens. In that clearing was where she found every nugget of wisdom ascribed to her. She kept telling them that wisdom was there for the seeing and listening. They spent too much time talking she thought. She knew they talked about her. Said she was a mad woman then and now. They called her Watta the Weird. She didn't hear them—but she could tell from their body language. She had perfected the skill of letting haters become background noise when she realised that listening to their chatter preoccupied her mind and stopped her from seeing the clearing. It wasn't worth it.

OrYa the Outrageous sprang up. She loved the talk and debate that happened at gatherings. She was determined that the traditions of old will not get lost in all the foolishness of this new wired world that she did not understand. Life didn't have to be so complicated. It was all very simple, this being alive thing…if only people on all sides of the Divide would understand that! One thing she missed was the pomp and pageantry of such events on the other side. She has crossed over while sitting outside one evening in a simple t-shirt and Ankara wrap lappa around her waist. What a way to make the crossing. She wished she had a big and bold headwrap with which to punctuate her arrival with an exclamation mark at the gathering. Her aura will have to do. It's all there was to work with on this side

On days like this Uncle Gassama the Griot was even more thankful he had his ceremonial stick in his hand when he crossed over. God knew he could not have been able to settle in this place if he had arrived without it. He would not know himself if he was stripped of his roles as head clansman and historian. He looked up and said thanks again. He felt a wave of love and saw the nod in response back. It was so good to be so much closer to God but sometimes, like today when they deliberated and searched for answers, it could be frustrating. He wondered if today's gathering would bring alignment or enlightenment, bitter argument or impasses. He sighed. He was beginning to wonder whether this practice was even worth it, whether any of it made a difference.

Then he was reminded of those whose clans were scattered. Those whose peoples did not deliberate for them. They are always lost. Adrift. Ships without anchors. On the other hand, for those whose clans gathered, whether they reached resolution or not, their people seemed to figure out living through the most difficult circumstances. Their roots were solid, their trunks of life unwavering. It made no sense to him, but obviously God had a plan for everyone, in all the eternal spaces. He shook his head in wonder as he felt another wave of approval. Duty called.

Musa, the Majestic tried to rouse Hassanatu the Harmonious.

"My dear, will you not even arise for the gathering. Will you never stop crying and fighting?"

She ignored him, continuing the digging and banging motions she had taken up once she was over the initial shock and it had sunk into her spirit that they had crossed over. The denial that she could no longer reach and communicate directly with the other side had never left her. She refused to learn the ways of this place. Refused to engage even with her own people. She spent all her time trying to break through the Divide. Time had not yet taught her it was fruitless. Musa the Majestic had appealed to the Timekeeper to help her. He had asked God to lift her agony. They had both given him the same assurance. Let time do its work. Leave her be. He had been waiting for a gathering like this though—hoping that the coming together of her own will move her. He watched her rocking back and forth, searching, peering through the Divide. He started reaching for her and realised his touch would be unwelcome. He rose to his full height and floated away.

Tity the Tiny floated giggling towards the gathering. This made her so happy. She loved being among the people. She longed for more gatherings even though she knew they sometimes meant there were emergencies on the other side. She should feel guilty for being so selfish but she didn't. She followed the town crier's voice, dancing, singing, skipping and clapping to the *akra* beat with her imaginary playmates They were all there when she arrived and took her spot. She loved that the drawing they had made for her sitting place was a tiny throne to match the other beautiful thrones drawn in the circle. She had seen other gatherings where the place mat for the

Tinies were blankets or cribs. She did not like that.

Gassama the Griot started off the proceedings:

"I am here representing the uncles and traditional guardians"

Orya the Outrageous piped up:

"I am here for the aunties!"

Tity the Tiny followed:

"Representing the children!"

Watta the Wise simply looked at each of them piercingly and grunted. They all knew she was there for the grandmothers. Musa the Majestic spoke up:

"I am the father of course. Hassanatu will not come."

There was silence…collective recognition of Hassanatu's sorrow. Wuzainatu the Wild stepped forward:

"I will sit in the place of my twin—is that not why we were born together and I found an excuse to make the crossing after she left?! I am here as the mother."

Gassama the Griot looked around and said:

"We are not complete without a representative of the grandfathers. Shall we proceed without one?"

There was a pause—then Sorie the Surly stepped forward from the witnesses who had spontaneously gathered to listen to the gathering.

"Fine! I will join in! This is such a waste of time—let each one figure out their own lives!"

No one answered him. They all knew it was a waste of time to reason with him.

Gassama the Griot continued:

"We are here, because our own child, Assanatu Kargbo is in distress. Her tears have touched the Divide…"

Orya the Outrageous interrupted: "Our own child! If she were our own child, she would use her real name! These children of nowadays are lost! Ana! Maria! What happened to Assanatu and Mariatu! When you cut your name, you cut the meaning and blessing ascribed to you. How is anyone to know that Ana is the daughter of Hassanatu, Granddaughter of Hassan, Great Granddaughter of …"

Wuzainatu the Wild interjected:

"Stop your nonsense Orya! We are not here to listen to your rants. OUR child is in distress, no matter what she calls herself. Will you stay in the gathering to help, or would you rather leave?"

Orya the Outrageous turned away from Wuzainatu the Wild and opened her mouth to continue, but then Gassama the Griot joined back in.

"We will focus on the issues of concern here. What is our daughter to do? The decision before her is not simple. Whatever she decides will determine her future and fate."

"Exactly!" piped in Sorie the Surly. "So why are we even here talking and pretending like we can change anything! We behave just like we did on the other side, even though we have a better view here and can see that the One Above moves the chess pieces. What idleness! This is why I used to sit behind the hut and refuse to attend the clan meetings…"

"You foolish man! You are just as foolish now as then! You think we women did not find out that you used to go look into the pots still on the fire and scope out the meat from the stews we had left to simmer while we attended the meetings? You are so lucky you were considered a big man of the clan and we children could not reprimand you back then. You have always been foolish because everything has always been decided for you. Can you not see the influence across the realms when we choose to meet and when we choose not to? Do you not see now how God is paying attention to what we are doing? Just open your eyes and look up!..."

Wuzainatu the Wild was out of her seat, standing across from Sorie as she wagged and pointed her fingers at Sorie the Surly. Orya the Outrageous was nodding and clapping alongside her in agreement.

"Enough!" Gassama the Griot shouted. "We accomplish nothing by yelling at each other! And just because we have equal voice on this side does not mean we will disrespect each other. Again, the question: What is our daughter to do?"

Silence fell over the gathering. On the other side it would have felt like 10 or 15 minutes, but for them it was just a moment of stillness in which everything came into clearer focus.

Tity the Tiny spoke up.

"Which option will mean that I get to have some brothers and sisters?"

There was a collective sigh and some murmuring among the witnesses.

Orya the Outrageous stood up, straightened her lappa and cleared her throat.

"My child" she started, addressing Tity the Tiny, "the truth is that we have no guarantee. In the stillness, this is what I saw, I saw that with the one called Brian, she will lack for nothing. She will live in great comfort. I saw them going everywhere in the canoe that flies through the skies. Ah! How wonderful the world has become! In the country that has the god that stands over the sea with her hand holding the staff up in the air, there are so many peoples. Some like ours, others like the pale people who came across the seas to visit us with skin all over like the palm of our hands. The women, their hair flies in the wind like kite strings—I wish to touch it! I saw them going to places where the buildings touch the skies and the clouds fall like powder instead of rainwater. In other places, people fill the streets, like car and lorry traffic in the cities. They walk so fast, it made me dizzy. I kept worrying they will crash into each other, but they never do! It's confusing to me though. They never walk far like we used to and they don't joke and laugh with each other or tell stories to each other. They all look so upset eh…and their eyes are just focused on the machine they use to talk to other people—but not the people they are with. Ah God!" she called, looking up: "when will you end the madness!"

"I also saw that Brian, he prefers her to be home like we used to, instead of how she is now running around with the men like a chicken. She no longer pushes paper after their first few years. He also wants her to keep making herself like a maiden preparing for marriage." Orya the Outrageous continued. "When she grows old, she is so beautiful, but he keeps paying with the trading paper and sends her to the medicine man who when she leaves his place, everything is like new again oh! Even her breasts are returned to looking like ripe fruit. I do not understand why he wants her to look like that in old age. If the lemon never gets squeezed, how will you gain juice for preserving life? What I did not see in their picture is any children or grandchildren, but to be honest when I was watching them go visit the place with the sign T-A-J M-A-H-A-L, hey—my eyes were open wide, wide so, enjoying the gold and the women's fine clothings…then I realised I had stopped following them…I had stopped seeing…" she ended sheepishly

Sorie the Surly, picked up. "I also saw no children or grandchildren with the one called Brian. And I see he spends all his time behind the machine that they write with. He is always drinking their own *ataya* brew which is black—but they do not brew their own, they buy it from the stand with the sign: S-T-A-R-B-U-C-K-S. His servants to, are never happy. When he calls them to attention, they are scared. Their chests are pounding like when the chief used to call the clan judgment circle and you know you and your friends are the ones who went through the farm plucking the best fruits but you are standing straight and looking the uncles in the eyes so they won't see you hiding the fear inside you. That is when the fruits can be turning in your belly and you will be praying for Allah's forgiveness so they won't come running down your legs to report you!"

Watta the Wild chucked: "Eh, even now, are you sure you did not go hovering over the place with the sign M-C-D-O-N-A-L-D-S, dreaming how you would have been licking pots there instead of following the stillness and watching our own?! Eh—monkey doesn't change its black hand—even across the divide."

Gassimu the Griot gave Watta the Wild a stern look. She stared back at him, but obliged and fell silent. He added:

"My own worry is the ending of our traditions and customs, of what has sustained us all the generations on the other side. See now how you see no children in that line—it is becoming the way. Our women no longer wish to marry and not all of them want children even if their bodies allow them to have them. They hold no naming ceremonies, they bring no kolanut to the elders to seek advice. Just like our own Assanatu's sister Mariatu, they do as they please. They marry the pale-skinned people and lose everything that makes them our own. Mariatu has done so. I do not want this for Assanatu."

Orya the Outrageous interjected, her voice unusually quiet—a thoughtful whisper as she said:

"My own Griot, I used to agree with you. I used to be boiling with anger listening to our own and watching them laugh at what we used to hold sacred. I almost stopped coming to gatherings for them because they had joined the pale-skinned people in considering us backward and taking on traditions that helps them lose all their own customs and identity. They no longer even dress in our beautiful clothes. They were causing me shame. Even this our own Assanatu we stand here for, I remember crying on this side when she joined the other young people, walking on the streets and asking people—strangers!! —to join them to tell our chiefs that we must stop our bondo society. They called it FGM—did she not know I was the head of the women's society, in our village. They denounce our customs, yet they were taking on the customs of others that are also not good for them —like living in isolation, which is not our way."

The whole gathering and witnesses were drawn-in, enthralled by her speaking, so she continued:

"Then I came to a clearing and was urged to listen. I heard at the meeting they called 'fighting for the African Girl,' our own daughter was standing in front of so many other men and people talking to the crowds about how to make new rules to keep girls safe from misfortune and *wahalas*, we considered common. She shared the stories of girls whose chests were just budding and had not even had their first blood being forced into and torn open. I remembered Bintu who we never spoke to as children after it happened to her. We all knew Papa Morlay had done it to her. No one would marry her and she always smelled because she never healed down there. I remembered my companions whose cuts were crooked and jagged who were always in pain—and never bore children."

She paused, gulped air and continued:

"When I heard them explain what happened in those cases, I wept. Remember when we used to think Albinos were devils and we used to stone them! Now, look what our children have learned and how that is beginning to get better. Look at all the ones we have met here, just like us! Now, I believe we must all be willing to learn. We must relinquish the things we did without full understanding, but the children must understand and keep what's important. If our own learn to do this, they will be fine no matter who or where they marry. They must not judge us unfairly by what we did not understand and they must honour what was the wisdom in our practices. We did not know."

Watta hissed her teeth

"psssst! Sometimes we did not want to know!! Some of us raised questions then but no one would listen. When I asked sister Mabinty to explain Bondo Society to me did she not call me demon child and beat me with these lashes that I will have until we cross to the final place? When I told our mothers that Chief Tholu forced into me, they called you there, Uncle Gassimu. Your edict was I should be silent about the matters lest there becomes a rift between our clan and the chief's and we lose our trading rights with them. I was sent to the women to give me herbs to drink and sent away to live at the missionary compound, while you all continued to lick his salt and eat meat from his food tray. If it were not for my twin Hassanatu who felt the pain with me and walked to meet me at the compound every week to console me, I would have been cut off from our people completely. I wish it was in this age so our own Assanatu could use the new rules to make him pay for what he did and I could at least have the medicine man explain what was broken in my body after that happened. I know that is why I could not bear children. I know that pain of childlessness too well, that is why I prefer the vision I see with the man Oluado she will meet if she takes the acceptance to go learn more in the other city."

"Ah, I like that vision!" Gassama the Griot concurred. "He is not of our nation but our customs are so similar! Their lives are full of the bounty of children, grandchildren. There is much laughter in their home and they do naming ceremonies! They attend so many community events. The children do live like the pale-skinned, but they also know our names! One of them even makes many trips home. He goes to all the places we lived, even the places now full of concrete buildings, he writes our names down to 7 generations past and hands it to his own child to continue building the tree of our names!"

"I agree!" shouted Orya excitedly. "It is an amazing life with this Oluado. They do not have as much trading paper as she will have with Brian, but theirs is a good life and they do make many trips in the metal bird too!"

Tity the Tiny chuckled, nodding vehemently and an excited chatter arose among the witnesses.

Musa the Majestic arose. His presence was enough to slow the excitement—like when a rush of wind meets something in its path that causes it to change shape and slow to a hush.

"I have heard all your thoughts and saw what you have seen, there is one thing about that vision that has not been spoken. Yes, Oluado will love her, but my own Assanatu will not accomplish some of the rulings and laws that will keep our children safe and accepted—both those that live in faraway lands and those that live at home. She will accomplish much for her family and she will continue to work and serve. She will strengthen her community and motivate younger ones from all over our forefathers' lands in Africa to stand proud. But she will not get the seat on the committee where all the international rules are made. She will have left that chance behind when she leaves her current place. Hers is not an easy decision. Many lives and fortunes depend on what she will choose. That is the agony she feels. The work that's needed will eventually get done, but it will not be done by her. She will know this in her heart and soul and part of her will always be longing for what she could have done. She will feel that she missed an opportunity but I did not see what that opportunity is."

Watta the Wise unfolded from the crinkled position she'd

seemed to be it and opened into a beautiful form—like an origami, she seemed to be able to shape-shift beautifully. Her otherworld-ness was both foreign and attractive to them. She beamed at Musa the Majestic:

"My child, you have seen clearly. Thank you for listening deeper. Beyond that, there is one more option and that is what you have begun to see, my son, but that was not all of it. In this final case, she ends with neither Brian, nor Oluado. She does not accept the new learning opportunity now, although she will learn even beyond that later. If she chooses this path, tomorrow she will go see the one she now serves called Phillip and explain to him that she can serve him no more. They do things that cheat and steal from other people. The one called Phillip will deny it all and she will leave that serving place. She will then start a new place of her own, and she will hire all our own people from many different nations of our forefathers, who have been working for others like Philip but not rewarded. The Philip masters are dishonest farm owners, without scruples. They are those who will give their farm workers the worst of the produce and even steal from the poorer ones they are supposed to be helping until their barns of trading paper are overflowing. Yet, they will continue to take from others who do not have. Her own farm place will do well. There will be challenges when some of our own want to behave like the Philips they have left, but she will remain strong. It is from this that the opportunity you saw that she will miss by leaving now and meeting Oluado will arise."

Tity the Tiny floated over and tugged on Watta the Wise's form:

"Great grandma," she said "when you were talking, I saw the picture of it. And I also saw children in the picture but you do not speak of children?"

Watta the Wise enveloped Tity the Tiny and said: "My precious, there ARE children. Your mother will take 2 children to care for as her own from our own country when her moons for having children passes and she has not married or found a companion she wants to bear children with. She will also have 3 more children, who will belong to the man she meets many moons from now and marry in her older age. This man is called Xavier. His father is from one of our forefathers' nations, though not our own and his mother is of the pale-skinned peoples. They will have both accomplished much for the world before they meet and together, they will be happy with their 5 children and many grandchildren. When these cross here, for sure you will be part of them. The only difference is that gatherings for them must happen first by those in the Divide of their bloodline and only if those do not gather for them can we choose to. However, remember, that if this is the destiny she chooses, you will be the most delightful surprise waiting here for her when she crosses the Divide."

Tity the Tiny snuggled into Watta the Wise's folds, content with what she had heard. Musa the Majestic looked to Watta the Wise: "So what shall we choose? For me, I would like it to be what makes her the happiest AND fulfilled."

Gassama the Griot exclaimed: "Shall we put our children's happiness above tradition and legacy?!"

Watta made her way to the Centre, still encircling Tity the Tiny and with a voice of steel that signalled finality said:

"We will not choose for her! ***She*** will choose. We will learn as Orya has urged us to and let her decide her own future. We know that if we choose in this circle, she will be swayed that way and that will cause her more distress, because she will know that she has been swayed by the parts of us still living in her."

Watta the Wise reached into her bosom and opened her palm to reveal one of her prized kolanuts. A hush of awe rippled from the gathering and rolled over all the witnesses. Watta the Wise had been carrying those kolanuts of welcome when she made her crossing. It is said she knew it was her time and had packed as any as she could into her bosom to bring them to this side as a continued symbol of peace, welcome and the bitter sweetness of having lived, yet having to leave to make the crossing to the ancestors. When any of her own arrives, they receive a kola nut from Watta the Wise once they realise they have crossed over.

Now, she placed the kola nut in the Centre, where the edicts of all the other traditional rulings from their previous gathering decisions resided. The kolanut sat on top of the older edicts like a crown. Watta the Wise said:

"This kolanut symbolises that whatever our own Assanatu Kargbo chooses, she will be at peace and as our Musa the Majestic has asked, it will be what makes her the happiest and fulfilled. We here, will also remain at peace with her decision" She then glided through the gathering, kissing each one of them on the head, and then floated away with Tity the Tiny now fast at rest in her bosom.

One by one by arose and departed to their corners in the Realm. When Musa the Majestic got back to his space, he could not believe his eyes. Hassanatu the Harmonious was leaning against the Divide, fast asleep and smiling. It was the most peaceful he had seen her since they made the crossing. He heard a gasp behind him and turned to see Wuzainatu the Wild. She had arrived for her daily session of sitting beside her twin and weeping with her while trying to convince her to stop crying because all will be okay on the other side. They stared at each other in a moment of confusion. Then clarity dawned on them as they realised that what they had just experienced had also reached Hassanatu the Harmonious.

~~~

The alarm went off but Ana was already awake. She had been up for about half an hour, staring at the ceiling, reflecting on her dream. It was the wildest dream, but she felt strangely calm. She had gone to
~~~

bed expecting to wake up with a headache after her breakdown last night, but instead, her head felt clearer than it had since…well, since her parents died. She knew she needed to get up, make her coffee and get dressed for work. She had a pressing file to work on too, but she couldn't get herself to move as she savoured the images of seeing her Dad and favourite crazy Aunty Wuzainatu in her dreams. There were a few others that she didn't know but they all looked familiar. She couldn't hear what they were arguing and talking about at first, but eventually they all seemed happy and peaceful.

The best part was that Mom was standing as if at a window with her palms against it. Ana had pressed her palms against the glass and that's when she had seen the others. Mom looked more serene and happier than Ana had ever seen her in life and her eyes said: *You're going to be okay.*

She thanked God again for whatever the dream was meant to be. Certitude washed over her like a warm bath. She knew what she wanted to do. She thought of calling Maria to tell her about the dream, but she didn't want Maria to think she had finally lost her mind to her grief. Instead, she reached for her phone and sent Adama a message:

> Hey Bff: I know what I'm going to do. It's going to be a crazy day because I'm going to have all the conversations and make all the calls today…and no, I won't call to update you first because I don't want you to change my mind! About to turn off my notifications 😊. Let's meet to celebrate at mine over wine tonight, ok? P.S had a crazy weird but good dream of my parents last night. Will tell you about it too. Ttyl.

6. OPEN ADOPTION

An open adoption is an oxymoron when your skin is like mahogany and the rest of your family are encased in white pine. I checked the box for African descent/Black on the forms we were filling, involuntarily shrugging at the sound of Mom's voice in my head saying: *you can find out who your birth parents are anytime. The adoption was open and I have contact details.* My sister was beside me checking off the box for Caucasian. We called ourselves family, but people never failed to remind us and point out the obvious. I expected it. I could even sense it coming. Yet I was still surprised whenever it happened.

We went to the desk to return the forms.

"Mary Grey?"

"Yessir, Plain old Mary Jane Grey here!"

My sister had perfected making fun of herself so others wouldn't. I couldn't understand why she did that. She was gorgeous by any standard but refused to believe it.

The agent moved his eyes from the photo on the form to my sister's face a few times, signed beside her photo and placed it in the bin beside him with the label: verified.

"Ma-li-ka Grey?"

"It's pronounced Ma-lie-e-ka. And yes, that's me."

"What kind of name is that?"

"Her name!" exclaimed my sister.

I shot her the look that said: *please don't make a scene!* She paid me no mind. She glared at the agent who at first returned the glare, then started turning red, shrugged and turned back to me. The agent repeated his head bob to compare my likeness to the photo on the form, but after his first gaze, he flipped my form over, reading out:

"Born in Greece?"

"Current citizenship, Canada?"

"Citizenship at birth, Sierra Leone?"

I nodded each time, wondering why each is punctuated with a question inflection rather than a period for the statement of facts that they were.

"Ah! So that's where the name's from then—Africa."

I felt Mary about to explode beside me when I heard dad's voice saying:

"Everything ok with the forms, sir? I'm Mr. Grey—their dad." He must have decided to come in after finding a parking stall after all.

The agent looked up and smiled.

"Yes sir, just confirming details for your adopted daughter here." He answered.

Dad smiled the way he does when he's about to take someone down, like he did when he played American football. At the same time, Mary slammed against the desk. If I looked like either of them you would have seen me flush red, but instead, I hung my head, letting it fall limp off my shoulders and onto my chest. *Hang my head.* No wonder they called it that. I felt like dying in that moment so I could disappear.

"Which one?" Dad asked too mildly.

"Well…" the agent looked up, seeming irritated. "the African one of course."

Mary hissed "Let's go, Malaika."

I stared at the agent, shook my head and followed Mary through the line-up and out the doors. The people close enough to have heard what went on avert their eyes as we stalked off.

We stood outside waiting for Dad to emerge. Mary decided to sneak in a vape. We had a clean view of the glass doors from the pillar we were leaning against waiting for him to re-emerge. I said:

"You really should quit vaping. It's just as bad as straight smoking."

She grinned and answered: "Shut up! And how do you manage to stay so f-ing calm every time this shit happens?!"

"Because I have you carrying all the rage for me. You should also stop swearing so much."

She stuck her tongue out at me and threw her vape back in her bag.

"So sick of it."

"You should get used to it, girl. Been that way since we were kids and it's not going to change."

She stared at me: "It has to. It has to." She repeated, as if to convince herself. She came over and gave me a hug.

Dad was walking over to us— "come on girls, let's get out of here!" We fell into stride with him, which under normal circumstances was a feat. That day, he was so upset he was moving even faster. I added a skip into my step to keep up. I looked over. Mary was practically jogging.

"How'd it go in there?"

He grunted.

We said no more. We got into the car and sped off.

~~~

The car came skidding around the corner. The driver hit the horn, blaring the full ten yards leading up to the gate and leaving a trail of red dust in the wake. The neighbourhood Fulani woman who owned the corner store opposite the gate stepped out of her stall and yelled at the security post— "Amidu! Amidu! De mami don cam! Opin de gate!" *Amidu, the Madam is here, open the gate!*

She did not seem to notice or mind the dust shower she was being blessed with as she called out to the security guard.

The window of the BMW rolled down and a silky-smooth voice called back out:

"Good Evening, Jeneba!"

"Good Evening, Ma! God bless you, Ma" the corner store lady called back. The electric gate whirred open just in time for the car to continue its smooth sailing into the driveway leading up to the imposing house at the top of the hill.

The home was an African architectural beauty, featuring local and recycled materials from mahogany wood shutter panels to red brick and adobe, to raffia-designed overhangs and carved walnut posts integrating historical Sierra-Leonean facts and figures. It was surrounded by manicured lawns and beautiful flower gardens as far as the eye could see. A cacophony of red and purple hibiscus and bougainvillea; orange, white and yellow arrowroot lilies adorned the grounds. The back of the property featured community gardens and agricultural plots of local produce, vegetables and greens, as well as a chicken farm. Three times a week during the dry season, the front and back gates were opened and the surrounding community joined
~~~

the staff to tend the garden and yard and do a weekly harvest. The sun was going down now and the solar lights around the property were lighting up as the car pulled to a stop in the front courtyard.

William was standing in position in his silk and African printed tunic shirt worn by all the staff in different caftan variants.

"Good Evening Mr. William, how was the day?"

"Good Evening. Fantastic Madam."

"Did the tutor call Jeneba's children to join the math and code lessons today as I asked?"

"Yes Ma."

"And how's your wife doing now?"

"Much better, Ma. Thank you for the medical support Ma"

"For nothing Mr. William. It's part of your benefit package. You and your family have served us well. Where is Miss Grace?"

"Here am I, Ma"

"Here I am, say here I am. Is everything in order for dinner?"

"Here I am. Yes Madam."

"Thank you. And the children?"

"Downstairs in the computing room Ma. All finished their homework and finished their dinner since they are not joining you and your guests tonight Madam."

"Thank you. I'll go see them now. Please make sure the car is unloaded and my things put away."

"Yes Madam."

"And Miss Grace? Thank you."

Miss Grace delivered a half curtsy with a mumbled "thank you, Ma."

"No no, Grace. Look at me. Do it with more confidence. Like this. Back straight. Look me in the eye. Try it again."

Miss Grace complied, delivering a much stronger bow with a huge grin of satisfaction on her face as she said a clear, "thank you!"

"Much better." Serah replied. She was smiling now too as she headed towards the side stairs leading to the children's basement play area.

Serah was on the floor in all the finery of her African lace and wax printed dress, being regaled by the four children aged four to twelve, when David came bounding down.

"Hello Chérie" he said as he kissed Serah's head then shouted "how are my kiddos today!!!"

He got the response he expected. "Finnneeeeeeee" as they ran full speed to pile on him.

He's a good man. He's a good husband. He's a great father. Serah turned away busying herself with putting away toys as she felt the back of her eyes sting. The tears have been happening a lot lately, telling on her more than she could afford. *It'll only be a matter of time before he notices…*

Miss Grace appeared on the stairway and said.

"Sir, Madam, Madam Crystal just called. She said they are on the way. I can take the children if you need to change."

"Good idea. Ok kiddos. Nighty Night. Your mom and I are having adult company for dinner. Listen to Miss Grace and head to bed on time, ok."

"Yes Papa!"

"Shall we, Serah" he said—offering an arm and reaching to help her up from the toys. Their faces met as she stood up, greeted by "yucky!!!" and "No public displays of affection please!" from Davida, the sassy 12-year-old.

They all laughed and Serah and David headed upstairs.

As they went down the corridor to their bedroom on the top floor, David started rubbing the small of Serah's back and reached to nibble her neck. She smiled, gently moving his head and wiggling out of his embrace.

"No quickie for you handsome…I'm changing in the bathroom…it's that time of month…"

He groaned and let go…loosening his tie as they entered the room.

Crystal and her date Frank had just arrived when they came back down and the rest of the dinner party arrived in quick succession. They were North American and European diplomats and staff from various development and international agencies. David and Serah had been part of the reforms that saw all development agency work in Sierra Leone and the sub-region coordinated, designed and led by locals. They had taken on some of those roles in Sierra Leone as local serial entrepreneurs who had modelled the reforms they called for. They were well trusted and well liked—their dinner parties were renowned and that night was no exception. The laughter that ensued said it all. As always, the conversation turned to global politics and development issues and Crystal and Serah snuck away to relax by the pool.

"How's it going Serah? You are looking tired."

"I know, girl. It's getting hard."

Serah started saying "Did you…" when David's unmistaken boom rang out…

"There they are…what in God's name do you two always have to talk about!"

"Stuff!" Crystal and Serah said in unison, drawing laughter from David.

"My point exactly" David said, sidling up to Serah.

"Crystal, Frank is searching everywhere inside for you."

Crystal groaned, drawing laughter from David and Serah.

"Yeah—I have been wondering how you feel about him. He's very keen and seems like a decent guy."

Crystal answered: "I'm just not sure…let's see how we weather the next year when I'm mostly away and travelling. He's a nice guy. I'm just not sure how he feels about my passions and ambitions, you know? He's already complaining about whether I have to be away."

David said: "That partnership does matter. The next year is crazy for me too. I'll spend more time in North and South America, the Middle East and Asia working on trade deals and doing that one-year executive certificate program in international trade, patents and intellectual property law than at home. We've always made it work though, right, Chérie."

"Yes, we have." Serah responded. "I have been feeling sad about you leaving this time though. I have lots to keep me busy but I'm wondering whether I can do some travelling with Crystal too and help her with the new training for the Volunteers International missions in East Africa. I've never spent much time in that region either so it'll be a great opportunity."

"Hmmm! I see. Is that what you two were plotting about here?" David asked. His eyes widened, exposing a partly amused and partly contemplative gaze.

"Not even! This is the first I've heard of it" Crystal retorted. "You sure, Serah?!" Crystal looked uncertain.

"What are your thoughts for the children?" David asked Serah.

"We'll figure it out. Mama is coming to spend the year here already. It's actually the best time for me to do something like that. And I can look at business opportunities for us too..." Serah said.

"Yeah…it may be possible. Let's think it through in the next few weeks before I leave."

"Oh! There you are!" Frank said as he stepped out to join them.

~~~

We started cradling together with one of us curled into the other, back to front when we were 6 years old. That day, on the playground at school, Hamid, the boy from Egypt told me to "Go away! No one wants to play with a black girl like you!" That was also the day Mary started fighting for me. She was on the other side of the playground with the second graders but someone told her what had happened. She came over like a blazing tornado and delivered an upper cut to Hamid's chin before you could say: Hallelujah! All three of us sat in the Principal's office with Hamid nursing his chin and carrying on dramatically.

Our parents came by and all four got a talking to. Mom was livid, insisting she would talk to her daughter about hitting others but that more needed to be done to instil non tolerance for racial insults and microaggressions at the school. Dad was supportive but stood quietly by as always. When it was all done, the parents came out to get us. Hamid's mom came sheepishly over and quietly apologised to mom and dad and asked if she could hug me. Meanwhile, his dad stood reprimanding Hamid in Arabic until his cries got louder. Father Hamid then yelled Yalla! His mom let go of me in a hurry and followed her family out. Mary still doesn't understand why and how
~~~

Hamid and I became good friends in fifth grade.

It had happened before. This singling me out. In Kindergarten, kids had asked a few times why my skin was brown. I would just shrug, uncertain why it mattered or what I was supposed to say. In physical education and dance, we had to pair off once. At the end, the teacher, Miss Anne, looked around and realised I was alone and there was a group of three. She went over to the group of three and asked one of them to join me. Two of them insisted they had already paired up when little Suzie joined so Suzie was the one who should leave. Suzie started sobbing and told the teacher she wasn't comfortable joining me. Miss Anne looked confused and embarrassed. She tried talking to Suzie for a bit but as Suzie's sobs got louder, she gave up and said: "ok, I'll be your partner Malaika and you three can do the moves together."

Later, when friends asked Suzie what that was about, she said she was scared that if she touched me, she would also turn brown. Another time in assembly, when the school fundraiser for "Africa" was announced, everyone looked over at me and started giggling. Each time, I was confused but a few minutes later would be back at play. Except for the day Hamid insulted me and got an uppercut from my sister.

When we got home that day, I couldn't quite shake my melancholy. Mom and Mary kept trying to cheer me up. I stayed quiet. Mom read bedtime stories to us and tucked us in. She lingered longer than usual. She said a prayer, reminding us how special we were to God and to her and dad and that we should stick together no matter what people did or said. We nodded dutifully. Dad who had been leaning on the doorframe called out: "goodnight girls" and they left. We lay quietly on our single beds. I had my back to Mary instead of facing her and chatting like we usually did. She let me be. Eventually, I heard her rhythmic breathing fill the silence. I let go and started sobbing silently into the night, wishing the moon streaming through my window would take me away. I didn't hear Mary's breathing stop or hear her move. The next thing I remember is that she was curled up behind me and had snaked one arm around my body while the other stoked my head. We fell asleep together that way.

This became our ritual and was literally the way we had each other's back. It was the small hurts that only we recognised. Or the big ones that no one else, not even mom could console us through. Like after our 16th birthdays when mom told us about the open adoptions. Mary decided she wanted all the information and contacted her birth mother who was living in Victoria, BC. She agreed to meet Mary who rode the ferry from Vancouver's mainland to meet her. She was greeted by a beautiful petit brunette named Louise, who was well put together with perfect manicured nails and red toes shimmering out of her sandaled feet. Louise took Mary for a tour and tea at the Butchart gardens. She explained to Mary that she was glad to meet her, but that Mary had happened when she was part of the rave culture – young and foolish. She had no idea who Mary's dad was and was now happily married with other children. She had not told her family about Mary and wasn't planning to, but she would keep in touch.

Three emotional months later, after they had been exchanging emails and chats to Louise's anonymous accounts, Mary got a message.

> It has been great to get to know you Mary and I am so glad you have a loving and caring family. I cannot continue this double life. It feels like an ongoing deception and like I revisit the heart-wrenching guilt I felt when I gave you up for adoption to your mom that day 17 years ago. It is too hard for me and affecting my mental health and family life. I have made the hard decision to stop our correspondence completely. We leave for Australia in a week as my husband

has taken a job there. I wish you well.

Louise

When Mary tried calling, texting and messaging in all the ways she could, we realised Louise had blocked her number. A week later, all Louise's contacts were disconnected. That night, a week after the silence that followed Louise's note, I curled into bed with Mary, snaking my one hand around her and stroking her hair till she stopped shaking and fell asleep. We got closer and closer over the years. We were each other's best friend.

As we got older, it became clearer that questions about our family surrounded me, other than the exceptional time when people became aware that Mary was also adopted. Friendship groups became awkward. Living where we did, I was always the different one. Eventually, no matter how much I tried to fit in, the conversation became about me—where my birth family was from? How I washed my hair? And to Mary—what is it like to have a black sister? After a while, I couldn't take it anymore. I stopped hanging out with our friends. Mary understood. At first, she went alone, then she also stopped going.

Mom became concerned that we had no friends. She talked about it incessantly as she tried to make sense of it all, but dad said nothing. The more she talked about it, the more he remained silent. Once, when she thought we had gone upstairs, I heard Mom confront him: "why do you say nothing!"

"Because I always thought it was a bad idea." He answered.

"And I always told you that if you take me, you take her!" Mom had yelled back.

I realised in that moment that his silence was about me, not Mary, because mom had adopted me first and I was the flower girl at their wedding. I didn't want them to fight, so instinct took over and I walked into the room. They immediately changed the topic. I couldn't understand it. It started to make sense that Dad had always been kind to me but distant. What did he mean that it was a bad idea? I resigned myself to staying out of his way and his affections. But even Dad could not remain immune to the obvious insults. His silence was broken the summer day his friend Robert came for barbeque dinner. They had gone to high school together. The story goes that Robert wasn't the smartest, so after high school graduation he did that classic gap year, trying to make sense of his options. He backpacked across Europe, working odd jobs and eventually joined Teachers Without Borders, serving rural communities across Africa. After teaching in all regions of the continent—North, South, East, Central and West—Robert came home and ran in the provincial elections. He won, running on his global experience in a growing immigrant municipality.

When Mary and I came from school that day, and greeted Robert, his eyes lingered a bit too long over me. I made my way quickly back inside, shaking off the shivers running up my spine at his glare. After Robert had had a beer or two, he started talking nonstop.

"Your African daughter seems to be settling in well. How's she doing in school? You know, I taught so many of them all across the continent. They really aren't the smartest, so it's great that she's doing so well. Makes a difference that she's going to school here y'know…"

Mom went beet red and had tried to interject but Dad kept interrupting.

"Surely you don't mean all of them?!"

"That hasn't been our experience."

"What do you mean???!!

But Robert continued undeterred:

"you know, they grow up well though. I had my share on the continent." He was wearing a grin.

"And since, she's not really your daughter…I could come visit more…"

Dad stood to his full height, stared Robert squarely in the eyes and said:

"I think it's time you leave, Robert. And never come back to my house."

"Come on man, I was only joking!"

"And I'm not! Get out!"

That day, Dad joined Mom and Mary in becoming my ally.

Mom found a solution to her worries for us. She started taking us to support groups, talks and festivals. *For Adoptive Parents and Children. The Multi-Racial Family. On Racism, Race-Talk and Microaggressions.* At first, it was exhilarating to meet other families like us, but then two things made the experience go sour. First, I began to notice the looks of pity I got from the all-Black families. Once, a Black lady walked up to us and asked where I'd gotten my braids done and before I could answer, handed me a list of black hair salons. I told her I didn't need it. My mom did my hair. She looked stunned, muttered 'hmmmm!' and walked off. Second, I felt defensive and scared every time my family was referred to as part of the problem. *White Oppressors. Dominant Race. Complicit.* I started to worry: what if they felt insulted, or worse, inadequate and hopeless? They had been my only refuge…Mom insisted it was ok. She needed to understand the issues, she said. Mary and I needed to understand the sentiments that surrounded us when we were together so we are better prepared for the experiences we'd had, she encouraged.

At one talk for adopted children, everyone shared our

adoptive stories in the circle and Mary's story of Louise drew tears. After the tears subsided, the Black circle leader said:

"In spite of all that shared human pain, you do realise that you still have white privilege over your sister, right?"

I was sure Mary was going to breakdown even more and I was ready to get up and leave with her. Then I watched her eyes and saw her playing back the tape of all the times I'd been questioned or taunted, right beside her. In a quiet strangled voice, she said: "yes."

It was the Afro festivals that saved the day. We all enjoyed African music and beats from around the world. Caribbean vibes, Afrobeat, Samba and Afro Cuban music. As we participated in drum cafés and afrobeat dance, we started making friends. It was at one of those festivals we met Elodie, who became our third musketeer. Elodie was that Afro Brazilian with hair that every black girl who wore weave wanted. She was full of life and vivacious. She taught us how to handle microaggression in stride. Once when we were with her at a fundraiser, this guy who had been trailing us literally came over and asked her: what breed are you? I froze, while Mary got her upper cut ready. Elodie simply swung her Brazilian curls and curves in front of him and said: The Human Kind! Laughed and walked off.

Elodie taught samba and capoeira at Afro festivals. The day we met her, she was teaching and noticed how well Mary and I moved.

"Hola, sisters! I like your style, ladies!" After her class, she came over to us.

"Hey, they are looking for sisters to play masquerade on the carnival stage. One of the trios is a no-show today. Wanna join me?"

"But I'm not a sister!" Mary exclaimed.

Elodie laughed "The way you move! You her sister, right?!"

We both stared. No one had ever assumed that before.

"yes!" we said in unison.

"Then what ya waiting for. You in? Let's go change!"

When Elodie was done giving rapid fire Portuguese instructions to the Brazilian aesthetician dressing the carnival girls, we emerged masked as glossy and glittery temptresses, with feathered wings and golden see-through cat suits that gave away much, covering only our most private jewels, just in time. Mom looked both proud and amazed at our womanhood and horrified that we stood on the main stage in all our glory. I was sure Mary and I were about to make fools of ourselves. But when the music started, freedom coursed through our bones and we moved with the beat, all three of us, perfectly in synch as if we had rehearsed a million times. We won the first-place prize and mom screamed so loudly she lost her voice. When we got home, Dad was less than amused. "Once is good enough, girls. I'm glad I missed it and don't ever do that again!"

We promised we wouldn't, knowing we were lying.

~~~

"I can't believe you did that Serah!" I can't believe you're getting away with this!"

"Crystal, it's the only way. What do you want me to do? Go back to David and spill all? I'm killing two birds with one stone here. I really do need a break. If I stay close to him right now, I'll implode and that's not fair to him."

"You're crazy you know that friend?! You're going to drag me down with you too!"

Serah grinned and gave Crystal a hug.

"Too late now, honey. I'm already your problem."
~~~

"You are lucky I like you!" Crystal shouted above the plane engine noise as they walked from the shuttle onto the loading ramp, outward bound from Lungi International Airport to Jomo Kenyatta International Airport in Nairobi.

Serah loved Nairobi. The temperate weather agreed with her and she felt so much better than she had in Freetown in the past few weeks. She loved volunteering with Crystal and spent her evenings on skype or WhatsApp with David or with the children.

"You look well, Chérie," David commented after about three months of her time there. "And happier than I've seen you in a while. Nairobi agrees with you. Perhaps I can stopover to see you and Crystal on my way to Freetown to see the kids? I can reroute from London to Nairobi and then over to Freetown? Maybe we can both go and surprise the kids?"

"No David. We are off to the interior next week and I am meeting the business women I've been telling you about who are working with bitcoin and block chain. I miss you, but I need to do this. The next three months will fly by. We'll be together again soon."

He sighed. "Ok Chérie. I think this has been good for you."

"Yes, it has." She replied.

They said their goodbyes, with Crystal joining in to wave into the camera.

That day, after he hung up, Crystal looked intently at Serah and said: "Why Serah. What happened?"

Serah paused and sighed: "I don't fully know, Crystal. I only know that I was bored and have been for a while. And David…he's charming, he's amazing…but the chemistry is just not there and never was for me. I convinced myself it'll be ok because everyone told me I'd be foolish not to say yes to him. So I did, but it's cost me a lot. And when that Senegalese ambassador shook my hand, I realised how much it had cost me…"

Crystal remained silent, rubbing Serah's feet.

"I toyed with the idea of leaving but I know I can't. I'm staying for the children's sake, but I needed to do this for me. I've done everything for him and for the family. This, is for me."

The next day at the office, Crystal came from a meeting looking troubled. She had to go on a tour to teach European Aid volunteers, while exploring partnerships. She was to go to Turkey, Greece, Italy and Spain.

"I'll be almost eight weeks on the road. Will you be ok staying on your own?" Crystal asked Serah

"Hell no, girl! I'll come along. We'll be back in plenty of time for me to head home on schedule as planned.

"Are you sure?" Crystal offered, looking worried.

"Never been more certain!"

They left the next day, making their way through each stop successfully. Their last stop was Spain. While there, they heard from the partners in Greece. Some new possibilities had emerged and they were hoping Crystal would go back to meet key members of their team.

In the middle of the second set of meetings in Greece, Serah was taken to the hospital.

~~~

Mom's heart attack episode scared me. She recovered well, but the ordeal made me pensive enough that I finally asked for the details and contacts behind my open adoption. I travelled to Freetown in
~~~

awe of both my Moms and what they had pulled off. They had kept in touch as much as they could, and Mom showed me the notes Serah had sent in case I ever chose to connect with her. They all started, *My Angel, Malaika.* When I arrived in Freetown, I stayed with old friends of Mom and called Mom Serah. I assured her I was happy to meet outside her home. I understood the situation and after Mary's experience with Louise, I planned not to impose at all, and worked myself into being content with whatever Serah would offer. She insisted I go to her home. My brothers and sisters were all abroad studying, she said, and her husband was hardly home. It was safe to go by and she would send a driver to pick me.

I was thankful Mom had explained everything to me including the details of Serah's home. Yet I couldn't help wondering what my life would have been like if I had grown up being picked up by the driver and driven to and from the grounds we pulled up into, surrounded by all the black and brown-skinned men and women who greeted me with smiles. Mom Serah and I hit it off. There was no melodrama. No tears. She simply glided down the stairwell that looked like it went all the way to heaven and said: "Malaika, My Angel. You know that's what your name means right? You looked like one when you were born and the memory of you has saved me all these years. Come here." We embraced, then she pulled away and said: "Let me look at you. Crystal did a fine job. May God bless her and her husband. I know our…ploy…was hard for Frank to stomach and I don't blame him."

We spent the next few weeks visiting at home and running errands together. She introduced me simply as a relative from Canada. One day, we came home to be greeted by David. Home early to surprise Serah. Serah hesitated, then alighted to greet him with a smile and an embrace. I saw first-hand how much she had perfected the act of pretending to love him. I stayed in the car, uncertain of what to do until Serah called out.

"Malaika, come meet David."

I stepped out, feeling dizzy all of a sudden. My hands felt clammy as I reached to shake his outstretched hand. I heard Mom Serah saying – "Remember my cousin Lizzy who was born in Canada? The one we visited in Montreal about 25 years ago? This is one of her daughters."

David took me in. His eyes dilated and for a second I thought all hell was about to break loose. Then he pulled me into an awkward bear hug. He was about five-feet-four-inches, an inch shorter than Mom Serah and I was five-feet-seven-inches.

"You are always welcome here, daughter! Let me see, you must be about 20 years old, am I right?"

My throat felt like dry ash as I said "yes sir."

"I thought so," He said pointedly. "Please, call me Dad. Everyone does around here and you will meet your sisters and brother eventually."

"My sisters and brother!" I spluttered.

"Yes, of course. In your mother's tribe, there is no word for cousin, only sister. So, you shall be their sister. Let's go toast your arrival!"

In that moment, as I watched David's act, I realised he had likewise perfected his lines and the pretence that his Chérie loved him.

~~~

Mary and I skyped weekly. It was our precious catch-up time for me with her darling daughter MJ, short for Malaika-Jane, who was eighteen months old.

"It's been 2 years sis. When are you coming back?" Mary implored. MJ babbled, touching the screen and repeating Aunti Makaike Aunti Makaike.
~~~

"Soon sis. And when I come, you and MJ are coming back with me to visit. You'll love it here. And now that Chris is out of the picture it'll be easier for you…"

"Girl, he doesn't want anything to do with us anyway. I'm still up and down, though. I wanted MJ to have a stable home. None of our rejection issues you know."

"She won't! She's got us and Grandma and Grandpa. Better that than a drunken deadbeat dad!"

"I know…" Mary replied. "I miss you."

"Miss you too, chicka!" I saw her hesitate, so I asked: "what's up?"

She paused another couple of seconds, then answered: "I was missing you the other day…so, Elodie and I, we cuddled together, you know…like we used to."

Now I paused. Then said: "Did it mean anything more to you? You know, than just a comfort cuddle?"

"I'm not sure…I can't process…I've got enough issues Malaika." She looked like she was about to cry. MJ started to fuss and cry. She must have picked up her mom's mood on cue like they say.

"Breathe, girl. Go take care of MJ. Why don't we talk again tomorrow?

~~~

I was screaming

Intermittently, I could make out the silhouettes of people trying to console me. Mom Serah. Dad David. Miss Grace. Mr. Amidu. Even Jeneba from the corner store. Then blackness and my own screams bouncing off my ears.

Why don't we talk again tomorrow?
~~~

More screams.

I miss you!

Blackness I was sure I could never come back from engulphed me.

I'm still up and down, girl. I wanted MJ to have a stable home. None of our rejection issues you know."

An echo in my ears.

"I'm not sure…I can't process…I've got enough issues, Malaika."

Now, I, could not process. It was unfathomable. My sister. My near twin.

Looks like she'd been drinking. Could have been an accident. Open bottle of pills. Possible suicide.

I have no recollection of the weeks that ensued. Only that somehow, I made it back to Canada with Mom Serah holding me up. I was greeted by a broken Mom Crystal and Dad Frank, shrunken with grief. Why couldn't she just accept our love? You had it worse and you managed so much better? Why didn't she leave Louise's rejection behind?

The funeral was a haze. MJ clung to me like she had always known me. I asked for custody. Chris gave it freely and quickly signed the adoption papers with me. Getting with Crystal was a mistake he said. She was too troubled. He wasn't prepared to raise MJ. I had no further conversations with him beyond the paperwork. I couldn't take it.

I felt like I would drown myself and Mary's dead body with my tears. When it was done, I was numb. The only silver lining was watching my Moms reunite and Frank wave a white flag to Mom Serah with his kindness and hospitality throughout her stay.

Mom Serah left before me reluctantly, but knew I had to wait for MJ's papers. I planned to return to Freetown with MJ. I had settled into life there slowly but surely. I had started an innovation and technology lab and had funding to get it off the ground. And there was a man. Mom Crystal and Dad Frank were supportive. When all was done and settled, they would come visit too, they said. That is where they had met after all. They took MJ and I to the airport on the day we left and bade us farewell at security.

An hour later, I called them to pick us up again. I had been held back and interrogated until we missed our flight. The immigration officers could not understand why I was adopting a brunette child to take to Africa, claiming she was my sister's child! They double-screened her documentation and I could tell they contacted immigration before letting me even make a call. We would fly out the next day and be greeted with extra questioning again at Gatwick airport before boarding to Freetown, Sierra Leone.

In Freetown, one of the first questions that greeted us was:

"Ousai you pull wait-man pikin!" *Where did you get a white child from?*

I wondered if I'd made the right choice. I talked to Mom Crystal and Dad Frank about sending MJ back. They refused— "she belongs with you, like you belonged with us."

I watched MJ's brunette hair blowing in the wind as she played with the neighbourhood kids. She was the gift Mary had left me. I was at peace. I somehow knew that on her way back to the West to find Chris who will ask for her forgiveness, and Louise who will be alone in a senior's home at end of life with no family visiting until she shows up, she will be just fine. She will simply be that white girl who happened to grow up in Africa.

7. SHADES OF LIFE AND LOVE

Every morning when he woke up, he liked to stand outside their home, close his eyes and feel the morning air. This morning felt crisp. Like the cassava flakes mama sells with the leftover fish they brought home from the fish wharf. His kept his eyes closed and gulped in the wind to help wake himself up, raising his nostrils to see what else was in the air. He smelled the smoke from the cooking fires being started. The women were waking up and soon the clamour of their voices will ring out, first distant, then loud as each household roused. The chickens had already started their morning call. *Cocorioko! Cocorioko!* The birds were answering: *We're Up! We're Up!*

He could smell the sea. It beckoned as always and he started walking down the path towards the sandy shore, kicking pebbles and sand as he went. There was no one on the horizon yet except the lone old man in the distance who was always there before him. He walked to the edge of the sea taking in the expanse of it for a moment. He never tired of staring at the vastness or listening to the crashing waves of the Atlantic Ocean. What are you saying this morning? He asked. There was no answer.

He went over to their fishing boats and started examining the nets that were hanging to dry, sweeping off the larger pieces of debris that were still caught in them. Just then, he felt the gush behind his eyes rolling in like the waves. He tried to fight it, quickly gulping in a huge mouthful of the morning sea air, but it didn't calm him. Instead, the feeling of drowning returned. He succumbed and started weeping again. He banged his head against the side of the boat in frustration as he wept. He didn't understand these tears. They came without warning, but only early in the morning like this or late at night when he was sitting out on his own. For that he was thankful. He couldn't bear the thought of crying uncontrollably like this in front of his dad when they were sorting the day's catch or when they were at the wharf bargaining the price of their bundles. He couldn't bear the thought of what his father might do or say. He told no one about the tears, because he was certain no one would understand them any more than he could.

He turned to the sea again. Can you tell me why I weep when there's nothing wrong? Again, no answer, so he started walking into the water. The power of the undercurrent pulled against his feet as he walked deeper in and he loved the sensation. It began to calm him and drew him further in. *Samba! Samba!* Finally, the sea calls! *Yes, I'm coming,* he responded. *Samba!* The sharp crack of the voice broke into his rendezvous with the sea. He suddenly felt a strong undercurrent pull. As he was drawn further underwater his arms and legs started working automatically as they had since his father started throwing him into the sea as a baby. He mustered strong strokes to angle away from the undercurrent, pulling just enough to be flung towards the shore instead of the whirlpool areas that they always manoeuvred around with the fishing boats. It was just enough to propel him crashing back onto the shore.

Abi stood there, hand on her hip as he swam the last strokes and arrived spluttering within yards of her. She took him in while he wiped moisture from his eyes and opened his mouth to attempt an explanation. She raised her finger and her stern look melted into a smile as their eyes met.

"Ar nor see natin sef," she said.

I didn't even see anything

He could swear their souls touched.

Then as she walked past him to rinse out the sandy tools in her bucket, she whispered:

"You know tiday, you nor know tomarra. Nor gree leh OLOSHORO kereh you go"

You know what today is like but you don't know what tomorrow may bring. Don't let the sea devil OLOSHORO take you away.

He didn't know why she had been at the shore early that morning, but he would thank the God the missionaries had introduced his family to many a time in his tomorrows that she had shown up. And he thanked the sea and OLOSHORO, for giving him back to the shore.

~~~

Manso had never been sure that he loved Tigidankay. He felt a deep sense of obligation toward her but he didn't know if that's what love was supposed to feel like. This love he saw around him in this place made no sense. People seemed to fall in and out of it so easily. Like his friend James.

Manso and James met on campus in his first year of university. They were unlikely friends, yet the perfect match. He, newly arrived from Freetown, Sierra Leone and James, who came into Regina from rural Saskatchewan. Manso noticed that the students from Regina treated him and James the same way. They ignored them—talked over and around them—as if, they were invisible. This, Manso noticed, was an amazing skill, given both he and James were remarkable on campus. James was tall and sturdy, clearly built and bred on a farm. He had striking hair which to Manso was orange but everyone else called red. Manso was not as tall as James, but he was
~~~

equally broad – a stockier version. He was also equally striking. It was 1948 on the University of Regina campus and he was the only black and African student in sight.

At first, Manso and James did not talk. Unlike the other students though, they did see each other. Perhaps it was the way in which misfits are sometimes drawn together magnetically. They would acknowledge each other with a nod in the cafeteria and Manso could sense that it was only a matter of time before they'd strike up a conversation. The way it happened though was not the way Manso envisioned. That day, Manso picked up his lunch in the cafeteria as usual and headed to his lone seat by the window. He passed James on the way and they shared their customary nod.

Manso was minding his business as usual, lifting his head every now and then to watch the other students and observe the abnormalities he still couldn't get over. There was the guy Bill, with long flowing hair. He wore it in a pony tail like a girl. He always walked with his girlfriend Suzy. Once they got their food, they spent the lunch hours kisses and touching each other all over at the table in the corner between food bites. Manso didn't understand how they could do that with no shame and how no one seemed to care. At first, he was disturbed that he was both disgusted and aroused by their public intimacy. Then after six months of watching them and others all over campus behave like that, he had become accustomed to it. He too, no longer cared.

Suzy had the writings all over her body that they called tattoos. This was the reason he had challenged the anthropology professor who had put a photo of an 'African' warrior man with tribal marking on his face and arms up and described it as a primitive practice of body markings. Manso had raised his hand as Suzy flashed in his mind:

"Please sir, I challenge that explanation. First, do you not yourselves have body marking practices you call tattoos? Would those also be considered primitive? Second, there is deeper meaning to a variety of body markings across the African continent. To understand the significance of these markings, we must first understand which country and which tribe this man comes from and then further understand the meaning in its cultural, customary context."

The class had gone silent. The air filled with a pregnant pause. Manso could feel the professor's steely gaze from under his glasses. He looked around the class, searching for support. Each student he looked at glanced away. He swallowed his confusion as his mind played back past discussions sparked by a student raising an alternate view. There normally was a buzz of follow-up chatter as others would chime in to add to what was said or throw in further challenge. The steely gaze he was currently receiving and the growing silence around him was not making sense. The hair on his arms stood on end as he braced himself. The professor finally spoke:

"Well then sir, why don't you enlighten us."

Chuckles broke out all around the class. Manso waited for their amusement to subside before he responded:

"I'm sorry that I cannot. Africa is vast and I have no idea which of her 54 or 55 countries, depending on how you are counting, that this person is from."

The chuckles petered out and the professor moved on to a picture of a Native Indian. Manso noticed that after that incident, he no longer made references to 'Africa' or used 'African' peoples again for his examples.

Bill and Suzy walked by, and then came Henry. Henry was the one who made Manso understand what book worm meant. Manso loved studying and learning but Henry was on another level altogether. His glasses looked like binoculars. He could barely see, yet he always entered the auditorium hugging a pile of books from his chest to his face. He had to look over the pile to order his food. Manso always loved watching Henry trying to decide if he should set down his books to get his food tray. He would look around anxiously, then finally decide on a spot he thought would be a safe distance to set down his precious pile and then quickly race to grab his food tray and make it back to his book pile. All while his backpack bounced on his back, clearly full of even more books. It was as if he thought someone was always chasing him determined to get his precious loot.

On that day, Henry got his food tray and after calculating his options decided to balance the tray and his books to walk to a farther spot, because all the spots close to the end of the cafeteria line were full. Henry's book pile was smaller than usual so making the trip across the room might have been possible. Manso watched with amusement as Henry did his balancing act. Then he saw it happen from the corner of his eyes even before it played out. Peter, the leader of the popular guys on campus crashed into Henry, sending his books, food and glasses flying. The gang surrounded Henry and started laughing as he fumbled across the floor grabbing each book he could feel and looking for his glasses at the same time.

Manso felt his blood heating up. He moved to help Henry, going over to retrieve the glasses that had slipped under an empty table. He reached for them, just as a foot landed between his hand and the glasses:

"What's up African monkey! You trying to rescue poor Henry! Who asked you!"

As if on cue, the gang starting calling out: "ooh ooh ooh eee eee."

Manso looked up and smiled. A sinister flash of white teeth as he said in a controlled clipped tone:

"You will remove your foot and let me take those glasses, or else I am about to make you a cripple. Then I will plead temporary insanity based on your insults and be deported back to my country, where I will live happily ever after, knowing your spine is broken and you can never do this to anyone, ever again."

That's when James appeared beside Manso and casually said:

"Brother, let me help you with that. Me, they can't deport."

His fist came out swinging, caught Peter below the jaw and sent him flying across the room. Manso and James stood together and surveyed the crowd. It was the uncanniest sensation. For the first time, they were being seen and acknowledged—with awestruck stares that were equal parts glares, fear and admiration.

The gang finally broke the moment by running off to help Peter who was groaning in the corner with what they learned later was a broken jaw. James and Manso helped Henry collect his stuff and get to his seat.

"Hi, my name is James, by the way"

"Yes, I know you are James. I'm Manso…your brother"

They had been inseparable since then, or as Manso described it the two of them, plus Henry, and whoever James was dating next became the misfit squad. It was like the girls who never saw them before couldn't stop approaching them since that day at the cafeteria. For each of the first three girls that James hooked up with, Manso was sure James was in love for real and would marry this one. They would be like Bill and Suzy—eating their faces everywhere. Then in three months came the fights. By the fourth month, they would have broken up and James would be tough in public and lament in private with Manso about how he was sure she was the one. This will continue until the next time that he'd again grab Manso excitedly to tell him he met 'the one!'

Manso became accustomed to this love pattern of James', and determined he would not be like that. Besides, he had promised Tigidankay he would marry her. He felt obligated to that promise. When Tigidankay finally joined him, theirs was a steady love. They were predictable, comfortable, but he had lived in this place long enough to begin to wonder if it was love at all. Then he worried that he was losing himself that he was now looking for this love thing that he already knew was temporal and explosive—like James and his women.

After James broke up with his second wife, Manso decided

this crazy love was overrated. That is, until the day he saw Tigidankay with Bakare, the guy from Ivory Coast. By then, he and Tigidankay had decided to break off after all—life was too bland. He thought it was for the best and didn't think he would miss her. Then he saw Bakare holding her hand and leaning toward her and he was ashamed and disgusted with the fact that his instinct was a balled fist. He remembers well when his dad used to beat his mom and he had sworn he would never raise a hand to a woman. His chest felt both heavy and hollow—like someone had punched a hole through it and left him breathless and struggling for air. It was unnatural to feel the rage that rose in his throat and choked him for someone you only feel a vague responsibility towards. He realised in that moment that he must love her, because for the first time he began to understand what James meant when he said he was hurting from a broken heart.

~~~

She considered leaving but they had come too far together. As they say in this place: The devil you know is better than the angel you do not know. How would she explain to her mom that she just left because they had grown apart? Her mom would never understand her reasons. She would only want to know: *"Is he a good provider?"* Yes, of course he was a good provider but her mom didn't account for the fact that she worked too—always had. Theirs was a different time — her mom simply could not comprehend why a woman would want to work when she had a man who provided for her. It's the same way her mom couldn't understand why she stopped having children after her second. And what would she tell those children, Matthew and Kaylee?

Matthew was extremely sensitive. He was tall, handsome and self-assured on the outside but his insides were easily hurt. He turned inward when that happened. Hidden in a cocoon of his own that no one could reach. He was like his father in that way. There were many times she thought she had lost him to his own world or worse that he would decide this world wasn't for him. It often happened when one would least expect it. As a child, when his sister told him she was smarter than him. In teenage, when the friend that was supposed to be his best friend moved and he felt rejected. When he won a
~~~

coveted internship, but had to wait a year for a placement and he convinced himself that his guaranteed spot would somehow disappear. She was worried, that even though he was a grown-up, he may not fare well with her news if she chose to leave.

Then there was her dear hot-headed Kaylee. She left fireworks or lit fires everywhere she went. She was that person who couldn't help but speak unfiltered. She called things as she saw them and said what she thought or felt. You either loved her or didn't. As a mom, she had hurt for Kaylee so much watching her grow up. She was the child who had all the friends or no friends and couldn't understand when no one wanted to play with her. She shuddered thinking about what Kaylee might say: "Mummy must have a boyfriend!" "Mummy just got tired of him." That, she could handle hearing, she realised. What she feared hearing was the truth, which had a way of coming out of Kaylee's mouth: "It's been a long time coming!" or "It's about time!"

She thought over the reasons why they should stay together. They had been through a lot. At first it was all roses. They were full of life, anticipation, and enthralled with their good fortune. They studied hard and worked hard. They never ran out of scholarship money. They survived that first winter when she felt like she had walked out of tropical heat into a freezer and would surely die of cold. They had landed work and placements right out of school, enabling them to complete their immigration process. They had worked hard through all the years of raising their kids. They had been happy. Those were the glory days.

Somewhere along the lines, this land of milk and honey became the ordinary hamster wheel of their lives. The milk was curdled and the honey became hardened and cloudy, reflecting the way their lives had become crystallised. They spent all their days just trying to stay on the wheel. And while they kept running, life kept happening. They had to cleave together when they lost his mother and her father. They held each other up when they thought their boy wouldn't make it after the skiing accident and through the difficulty of the rehabilitation process that had demanded so much of them. When it was touch and go, she had often found herself wondering how she would explain to her people what had killed him. She had resolved she'd just say he had a terrible fall—how could she explain skiing to those who had never seen snow? The pattern was always the same. Something in their lives would draw them together. Then they would drift apart again. She was so tired.

She checked the time. He'd be home soon and then she'll be leaving in 2 hours for the night shift at the hospital. She got up to start their dinner. Time for the same routine they'd walked through a million times it seemed. Small meaningless talk while they ate the jambalaya rice she'd cooked on the weekend and reheated. He'd be distracted about the paper he was working on now and talking about that. She'd pretend to listen to him while she cleaned up. Before she'd be done, he'll be back on his laptop and would barely nod at her when she said goodbye on her way out. *Oh well.* She sighed as she stood up to start heating the food. She switched on the TV and popped a Nollywood movie into the VHS. She loved the mindless distraction of the predictable story lines. This one was about the Princess who was sold out as a child to a pauper by an evil stepmother. It was clearly a Nigerian adaptation of Snow White.

She looked up to find him staring at her with a look she had never seen in his eyes. She yelped:

"You scared me! I didn't hear you come in!"

"I know," he said, his eyes soft and smiling.

She stared at him, uncomfortable by the attention of his gaze. She put down the bowl of food in her hands and reached up to straightened her wig. She suddenly wished she had paid more attention to how she'd look when he got home. She opened her mouth but he interrupted before she could speak.

"What time does your shift start tonight" he asked.

"Same time as always—7:00 p.m." she answered. He grunted, holding her gaze for a few seconds.

"Can you call in sick?" he asked.

"But I'm not sick! Why would I do that? I'm not sure what's come over you today but this is getting weird…"

"We need to talk. We need to work on our marriage. I would like us to go to counselling," he said.

She dropped the spoon she was holding. They stood listening to the reverberating clang. Tears sprung to her eyes as she held his gaze. Finally, she wiped her eyes with the back of her arm so she could see the dial pad to punch in the sick line number.

Five hours later they were still sitting over their empty bowls. It had turned dark outside but neither of them got up to turn on the lights. There was some anger and some blame, but mostly they shared their own inner musings and told their own truths in a way they never had before. The next day, they felt awkward with each other, like a newly dating couple getting to know each other again. They made it to the counsellors couch that day and for the next year and they never ran out of things to talk over. Even though they had invested 25 years, they were finally maturing together. She would always say that year grew them, and saved their marriage.

~~~

♪ *Then I think to myself, what a wonderful world! Yeah…I said to myself, what a wonderful world!* ♪

The whole room exploded in applause as the video documentary faded to a close. What a wonderful world was grandpa's favourite song. I looked over now and saw him wipe moisture from his eyes. I was so pleased to have touched him in this way. It was the best way to have put my documentary filmmaking skills to work. He was making his way through the crowd. He moved slowly these days but with no less presence than he always had. My gramps was always my hero and the 'biggest' man I knew, even though I had passed his height since I was sixteen.
~~~

My sister came over and we spontaneously high-fived each other. She had been my assistant on this project. My researcher and fact-checker. What a journey it had been for us to learn so much about Grandpa and Grandma.

"She's so beautiful and they are the cutest together!" my sister said.

Everything and everyone were the cutest for my sister, but on this, I had to agree. Our grandparents were the cutest. They were inseparable. Even now, Gramps had his hand on the small of Grandma's waist as he guided her through the well-wishers. It was an amazingly diverse crowd. From family and community to the friends from over the years of working in the United States, Canada, and all-over South America. They were glowing.

People came up to us too as we waited for the couple of the hour to make it to the front.

"Well done, you two."

"How powerful!!"

"Amazing storytelling and what great footage from everywhere they lived or travelled to."

"What an honour to your grandparents!"

"What a beautiful story!"

We accepted the congratulations heartily. My daughter, Diana, was starting to fuss in my arms. I started making my way over to hand her to my wife, but my sister tugged on my arm. I turned around to find Grandma signalling that I bring the baby to her instead. I nodded and headed back to greet them centre stage, with Diana in tow. I took the mic as they arrived:

"Congratulations on your 60th wedding anniversary Dr Manso Samba Kamara and Dr Abibatu Tigidankay Kamara! And happy 90th birthday Grandpa!"

Manso took the mic:

"I am overwhelmed" he said. His voice was breaking. Grandma looked at him with smiling reassurance as she now rocked Diana in her arms.

"To be here with my beautiful wife, friend and companion of 60 years, surrounded by our children, Matthew James and Kaylee Henrietta. To have been so honoured by our grandchildren, Samba and Abi—the ones named after us who made this journey retracing our steps from Murray Town, Sierra Leone to Regina where we studied and then all over Canada and America as I lectured and my dear Tigi served in various university hospitals. To see all of you, friends and colleagues who we have been serving with all across South America in these retirement years, here, to celebrate us! To be here, holding our great grandchildren in our arms! It is indeed a wonderful world. And you James and Henry! What a wonder that we are still in each other's lives. Although I am certain that these bags of bones of ours could no longer withstand a cafeteria fight if we attempted that one now!"

Grandpas James and Henry stood up and faked Karate poses just then, sending the room into fits of laughter.

Grandpa laughed through tears. He collected himself to continue:

"James, I am so glad you finally found the one! To your dear wife of the last 15 years – thank you for loving his insecurities away and sticking around with our unlikely squad, Mee-Yang."

Mee-Yang half-stood and blew him a kiss.

"Henry, thank you for sticking around tonight and not leaving to go read another book and work on your 1000th paper."
There was laughter again.

"And to you my dear Abibatu Tigidankay. You are the love of

my life. I have never forgotten that without you, my depression and hopelessness would have taken over and I would have walked into the sea that morning long before I knew of all the fortune in my future. You became my soulmate from that day. I went to the missionary hospital to ask for help because of you. And while I continue to critique colonial and post-colonial methods, it is the Methodist missionaries that educated me and it is through that system I gained my scholarship to University of Regina. You stayed with me through all my highs and lows and while at first I felt indebted to you for my life, I grew to love you fiercely. I thank that fool Bakare who tried to snap you away for opening my eyes! I cannot imagine my life without you and how glorious these latter years have been together."

Grandma turned and handed me baby Diana and reached over to kiss Grandpa. There was no dry eye left in the room.

"God has been faithful, my people. You all know of my Alzheimer diagnosis. I am thankful every day that my symptoms are stable and that today I remember each of you by name. My faithful Dr Abi here keeps me physically healthy and exercising and we will keep on as long as we can. All I ask now is if the symptoms become strong and I start to fade away, please, just keep playing me this documentary…over and over again…and keep loving and holding on to the ones you love. And on that note, let's dance!"

8. DEAR RUBA

"Catherine, would you please run my bath now? I'm done on the phone."

"Sure thing, Love. How was your talk with the family, today?"

"Great! No drama. No one is mad at anyone else…and my daughter and her husband…well, they're just so happy as always…"

"Ha! Let them be! Stop tempting fate. You should believe in love by now."

"I like to think I do…I like to think I do…so, what are we reading next?"

"*Eat Pray Love!* And don't even...!"

Mamie groaned and hissed her teeth.

Catherine laughed out loud.

"You can't do me like this, Catherine! Not another one of those ones…"

"My pick! You promised! You just made me read *So Long a Letter* and

I loved it! I would never have even noticed a book like that at a thrift store if not for you. What would you want us to read instead?"

"Glad you asked! On my list is *We Need New Names* by NoViolet Bulawayo, One of the Buchi Emecheta books I have yet to read or the newly released *Barracoon* by Zora Neale Hurston.

"Oh no no no!! A, I don't know the first two authors and I need a break from learning new African names and stories. B, I saw the news about *Barracoon*—it will be too hard for me to read in dialect so we literally would have to read and discuss it together, piece by piece. That'll be great actually, but not now. I'm emotionally spent and you know how those stories make me feel..."

"I know...which is why I make us read them." Mamie replied with a wicked grin.

"No can do! I need some *Eat Pray Love* this time. You know, we'll both enjoy it!"

Mamie stepped into the bath, muttering under her breath, "God Help Me!" even as her lips curled upwards into a smile.

She loved this unlikely friendship that had grown between them. This social experiment that neither of them would have dreamt up. Mamie, born in West Africa at the end of the 1920s and Catherine, born in Canada's Northwest Territories in the mid-1960s. Catherine was talking while she puttered around, laying out Mamie's clothes and medications. Mamie loved hearing her carry-on. She was saying something about *50 Shades of Grey and Vagina Monologues.* Mamie smiled at the memory of them watching those together. She leaned back, closed her eyes and just enjoyed being in the warmth of the water. *You can do that when your bones are jangling in the sack of your skin and you have nowhere to be and nothing earthshattering to do*, she thought. It felt like too soon before the water changed from soothing to tepid. She started pulling herself up, knowing that it would take her two full minutes to straighten out and step safely out of the tub. In those two minutes, the water will change from tepid to chilling. She felt temperature changes so much more acutely these days.

Catherine was still talking as Mamie reached for the towel, patting herself dry.

"Ruba started her period." Mamie interjected.

"What?"

"I said, Ruba started her period." Mamie said a little louder. She sometimes forgot that Catherine was aging too, even though she seemed so agile. Everything about Mamie's body had drooped and dropped except for her hearing and her mind, so sometimes she muttered and forgot to speak just a little bit louder for Catherine.

Mamie was about to repeat herself into the pause when Catherine replied:

"Oh wow – that was quick!"

"She's 11." Mamie said, mostly to herself.

Eleven…a lifetime yet to go… and that life was already taking its first bend out of childhood into the inevitable circle of life.

"I think I'll write her a letter."

"A letter? Why not have her over, have tea with her."

"Because, my friend, some things I can only say in writing but won't be able to say to her face."

"I can see that"

"And some things, she may not understand now, but in time, she will and she can come back to the letter and re-read it."

"That's a great idea! It'll be your own *So long a letter*!"

"Except mine will be short. You know how I feel about writing."

"I hope you aren't planning to handwrite it!"

"Unless you help me, my friend, I may well be."

"Na-ah! Time to use that computer Mina bought you. You learned to text and use Facebook because of Ruba, you can learn to type a letter. I'll turn it on tomorrow and get you setup in Word. You might be able to do talk to text too…"

"Now."

"What?"

"Now. I want to start writing now."

"Oh dear. It's so late."

"What else have I got to do but drink tea?"

~~~

Dear Ruba,

I was going to start with niceties but I will get straight to the point. I am not much of a writer but I know three simple things that I'd like to communicate to you.

First: You are beloved. I love you. This is the most important point.

Second: Life is a marathon, not a sprint. I am at the end of my journey and have much I would like to share with you, so that's what this letter is about.

Third: None of what I write here is advice. Take it or leave it, it is my story. A tattered, imperfect gift to you that I hope will help you on your way, for whatever lies ahead. No matter what unfolds for you
~~~

and no matter what you love or hate in the stories I tell in this letter, never forget #1. I love you. You are beloved. This letter is written with all my love.

So here goes.

Your mother told me you had your first period and the wheels of my mind have not stopped turning since. I am replaying and recalling so many tapes. Dusty black and white movie reels and clips from my life that I thought I'd forgotten! Really, I had just buried them. Archived because they were too painful or just seemed irrelevant at this stage of my life. Today, I realised they were just filed for this day. Because what I feel more than anything is an urgency to share with you the things I would have wanted someone, anyone, to share with me. The journey of womanhood. I wish my mother would have shared the journey with me. Now, in the crisp hue of insights that come with twilight, I know that she may not have ever been able to do so. In her times, they were not equipped to do things like this. I could argue that I wasn't raised for this either, having never received it myself. But I'd be lying. Experience has been my teacher and it has taught me that knowledge, especially in a woman's life, is power. That behoves me to tell.

Spring.

You are in the middle of the spring of your life. A season that I think of as the first 20 years of womanhood. What an exciting time!! Your spring started long before you had awareness, when you were just a speck in your mother's womb. There, you were nourished and grew until you were born. That is a day I will never forget. A most joyous occasion and so different from my experience of birthing Mina! I thought I would burst open as we stood gazing at you, smelling your freshness, counting your fingers and toes. Then, they asked me to name you, an honour I never expected. I cried and cried for joy! Then as I looked at you and look around, it came to me in one of my native tongues. My stepmother's language which I thought I no longer remembered. Ruba. *Blessing*. You were and still are a blessing in every way.

We have watched you grow. Babbled with you. Screamed along when you took your first steps. Agonised through your potty-training—you have heard how terribly stubborn you were in refusing to give up your pullups, hiding under tables and pooping in them so we couldn't get you to a potty in time! Then all of a sudden, it was your first day of school. We cried. We laughed. We all went to drop you off and pick you up. What a sight we were! I was relieved that every black and brown family and all the first-generation immigrants of all nationalities behaved in this same way. I felt vindicated that we were not crazy after all.

Now, it seems all of a sudden, you are blooming. Transforming into the beginnings of womanhood. Preparing to continue the lifeline of humanity. I am not ready! I am scared of what womanhood brings. Even now, I feel my heart beating a bit faster and tears are breaking free of my eyes. I have no right to be this fearful on your behalf, for your spring has been so different than mine already! Might I be crying for myself? For the parts of my spring that I wish would have been different? It may well be. But this is one way a woman's spring can go, so I must tell you.

My early spring years were not unhappy, but I don't recall being surrounded by love as you are. I was born Mamie Nafisatu Boima Kuyateh, to your great grandfather by his second wife, Subi. I understand that theirs was a strange union. Across tribal lines and a union of choice and love. Her family did not understand or support her marriage even though her new husband was well-renowned. He was a Muslim leader, a cleric. She came from a Christian home. Her family were intellectuals who maintained homes in Freetown and the southern provinces of Bo and Moyamba, with a line of sons who attended the Bo School and Fourah Bay College. He was an astute businessman who traded in cocoa and diamonds across the West African region before it was commonplace to do so. That's how I grew up travelling to Guinea, Senegal, The Gambia, Mali and Nigeria, all before age 10, because my father only travelled with his favoured wife, my Mama.

When we were back home in Sierra Leone, I grew up like any other urban West African child of the times. It was not yet commonplace for girls to go to school but I did go, much to the relief of my mother's family who were ahead of the times and sent all their daughters to school. In our family, it was my eldest sister and I only who went—the first daughters of each wife, along with our two brothers. Like most in British West Africa, we wore uniform to school and spoke and studied in English. When we got home, we changed, reunited with our other three sisters and ran off to Arabic and Koran lessons.

After our lessons, I was supposed to do household chores and work with the women in the kitchen like my sisters. Instead, I would find myself with free time to play or read alone. Later, I was told how my mama's favour followed me not only when it came to travelling, but in our home also. Apparently, I had once burned my hand while helping in the kitchen and screamed. My Papa yelled at everyone and even slapped my elder sister who was in the kitchen with me. No one included me in chores after that. We spent the evenings together though, playing games in the yard with the neighbourhood kids at dusk and listening to the elders tell stories under the stars when it was moon shine nights.

I say I don't remember being surrounded with love as you are in spite of all this, because my mama always seemed so distant. While we all hung around and played in the compound after evening prayers, she always stayed inside or sat on the veranda overlooking the yard and observed without participating. She only came out on the moon shine nights when my father joined in the storytelling. Her distance got even wider when Papa's third wife Zainab joined the household. I remember it well. The celebrations and festivities took a week and I was sure the seams of our homes in the provinces and then back in Freetown, would burst open with the number of people who miraculously fit into them for the daily ceremonies. I loved the daily goombay drumming and dancing!

My favourite part by far though was the Nikaoh or Muslim wedding ceremony, because us children were told to keep disrupting along with our older cousins who wore veils and came out as fake brides. Each time, we would be given gifts of money to encourage us to leave so the ceremonies could continue. I remember when Ma Zainab finally came out and unveiled herself. I was captivated by her beauty! She had the darkest skin and every feature of her face was proportional, almost like a painting. Her skin was almost iridescent. So shiny! That was the day I fell in love with my darker skin tones which I had inherited from Papa over the fairer skin of my mom. Then I remember hearing a suppressed sob, like when a child is pretending not to be hurt. I turned around and there was your grandmother Subi, weeping behind her veil.

I remember trying to understand Mama's melancholy but never being able to. I tried making her happy. I would hug her but she would barely give me a squeeze back before she'd shoo me away. Was this not what she signed up for? Two things finally helped me understand my mama's sadness and these are both part of a woman's journey, my love. First, I would later understand that after me, Mama never got pregnant again. She bore the sting of an unexplained secondary infertility in a society that didn't then understand it. Indeed, in today's world, it may be understood, but women who live with infertility are still unsupported, even viewed as broken or somehow incomplete. What a travesty! Second, when Mariama Bâ's

So *Long a Letter* came out at the end of the '70s and I read it, I finally understood! I had gone home for Mama's funeral that year. More than mourning her loss, I was mourning her sadness, her distance and the fact that I, her only child never had a strong relationship with her. Then I heard the buzz about *So Long a Letter* and the fact that it was about to be required literature in schools! What?! I was so excited. In my day, we read *Pride and Prejudice* and Shakespeare books only.

I got the book and read it on the plane home. (P.S. I've read it more times than I can count but Catherine doesn't know that so don't tell 😊) Wow! What a gift. It was like Mama was talking to me through Mariama Bâ from the grave! You see, what I understood that day is that we women are such fools in love! Like most of us foolishly do, I believe she thought her love would change Papa and that he would never again take or need another wife. I don't know what their conversations and agreements were about this or whether he ever promised he would never take another wife because of her love – parents did not discuss these things with their children back then. I do know that she could never accept Ma Zainab, even though she continued to be favoured in many ways in the household. The only difference between Mama and the protagonist Ramatoulaye in *So Long a Letter* is that Mama was the second wife to begin with, not the first! Yet, she still believed Papa would change! She couldn't see that love aside, she was a great asset to Papa because an educated woman from another tribe made him look progressive and won him many business deals at home and across the region.

A year after Ma Zainab joined us, I got to go to England with Mama Subi and Papa. I was so excited! First of all, Mama was happiest on these trips when she had Papa to herself and had the illusion of us as a happy nuclear family for a few days. Second, we were going to England! Shakespeare's land. The place where our Queen lived! And we were going to visit Buckingham Palace. When I think of my excitement and carrying on now, I cringe. I cannot imagine how it must have felt to my siblings! It's a wonder they did not do me harm like the biblical Joseph's brothers did. Instead, my dear sisters ran waving and jumping and screaming bye bye, bye bye as we drove off, headed to the airport. I was 10 years old. Little did I know that that was the last time I'd see our Freetown home for another 40 years.

We had a grand time in London. I loved the red double-decker buses and I sang *London Bridge is Falling Down* every day. I was so happy when we went there! I had sung the nursery rhyme all my life and knew it by heart, but it was only now real to me. I loved the childminding program I went to while Mama and Papa went about their business. We did so many field trips—Madame Tussauds, British Museum, The Big Ben. I made friends with Suzanna and Oscar, who I would remain connected to for life. A week before we were to leave, Mama and I took the train to Essex to meet my Aunt Natasha, who was her older sister.

Aunt Nash, as I got to call her, was so happy! She called me Tity, which means little girl in Krio. She had got me a dress with a petticoat, a handbag and a fascinator hat and off we went to children's afternoon high tea! The biscuits and pastries and scones were all beautiful and delicious and the theme was the tea party in Alice's Adventures in Wonderland!! Everyone is invited to tea as long as you play along with the games and riddles conducted by the Mad Hatter. Such fun. When we got back, Mama and Aunt Nash told me I will stay the week there because Mama and Papa had a busy week and couldn't drop and pick me at the childminders. I thought nothing of it, but when I said goodbye to Mama, I should have noticed that she gave me an extra hug and squeeze and even patted my cornrows before she left.

Aunt Nash was kind to me, but all I remember of the first

year in London when it sunk in that Mama and Papa were not coming for me was confusion. Papa talked to me on the phone after they were already back in Freetown and told me the same lies Mama told him. *It was only for a year so I could get some experience going to school there. They would come back for me then.* Mama refused to talk, said she wanted me to settle in first and get used to being with Aunt Nash. At first, I cried a lot. The shine of being in London was quickly replaced with the cold, grey, silence. And I had to start doing chores! I just wanted to go home to my sisters and brothers. When I saw that my crying was starting to make Aunt Nash mad, I stopped. I became very quiet and compliant as it sunk in that my parents had abandoned me in London.

I can't remember much about that first year or two there. I think my little mind shut down during that time. What I do remember is a lot of buzz and news about the dawn of the Second World War, amidst a set of bewildering personal experiences. It started when Aunty Nash and I went to an office a lot and spoke to a lady who wrote lots of notes. Then one day, I was taken to this British Family's home. I could have been there weeks or months, I don't know. The couple, Margaret and Charlie were charming. Margaret even knew how to wash, comb and fold my hair and told me she had had many children like me come through her home.

Eventually Aunt Nash picked me up again, apologizing profusely. *It was necessary*, she said. *It was necessary. One day you will understand. Praise God this worked out before everything shut down oh! Things are getting worse.* Later, I would understand that Aunt Nash had registered me as an abandoned child, spinning the story of my family as a hostile polygamous environment that I could not return to and seeking asylum and custody for me. She had to give me up to foster care to prove her story and eventually got full custody of me. And so, I became a British citizen. I also understood that it had been Mama's plan all along. When Papa married Ma Zainab, she had decided to remove me from our home.

My love, it was the day after I returned to Aunt Nash's home that I got my first period. At first, I panicked and started weeping. I thought I was ill on top of everything else and would never see Mama, Papa and my siblings again. Aunt Nash heard me and started banging on the bathroom door for me to open. *Tity, you need to stop this crying! We are doing this for your own good! Are you not back here now? No one has abandoned you. You will be fine. Open up. Open up, I say!* I opened the door. My underwear was around my knees with the blood stains in them and there was blood running down my thighs. Aunt Nash started crying and laughing and hugging me. Then she helped me clean up, explained it all to me and showed me how to use menstrual rags, something I am so thankful you never have to deal with, lovely Ruba! I still laugh at the sex education I got from her that day with stern eyes and finger wagging: *Don't let a boy touch you from now on eh! If you do, you will get pregnant! I don't want any trouble from your Mama and Papa.*

For weeks, I walked around refusing to let any boys in my class or neighbourhood even hug or shake my hand. How they must have thought I was crazy, especially since we were so often packed together during bombing raid drills and in the bomb shelters! Thank God that I was still able to correspond with Suzanna from my London childminding program. We were fast pen pals and though mail was slow, it still went through eventually. I wrote to her and asked if she had had her period too. We exchanged notes and she wrote explaining that her sister had told her that the touch was actually sex. It starts with a boy sticking his tongue in your mouth and then rubbing you all over your body. She said you get pregnant only if he put his privates into your body, in the same place where the blood comes out of. Her sister had been doing it with her boyfriend who had just been conscripted to the army.

I hope you are laughing Ruba, at the rudimentary education I had, compared to your life. I was so wowed by the puberty app your mom showed me last year that she got for you. It explains everything so beautifully and how I wish I had that back then! But c'est la vie. Life changes so fast. Look how far we've come! I know you do not need the lessons in anatomy and sex, so my purpose here is to share the life lessons that no app could ever teach you.

Anyhow, I thought the whole description of sex I got from Suzanna sounded so disgusting, that I had no interest at all in boys through my teenage years. It was a good thing, because we were occupied with surviving the war. Aunt Nash considered sending me to one of the children's evacuation centres in Cheshire because it was well-funded by the Americans. Children were being evacuated with their teachers and since she was a teacher, she could keep me with her, which was the only way I would agree to go. This is when I realised how much anxiety I'd developed over being 'abandoned' twice. I thought that if Aunt Nash and I were separated, I would never see her again. So, she decided to keep me with her. She had no shortage of work supporting the refugees pouring into London and the immediate environs from elsewhere in Europe, even as urban London children were being evacuated to the countryside. I learnt a ton, both going to school and volunteering alongside her until the end of the war. Then at 19, after finally finishing my Advanced General Certificate of Education after the war adjustments and delays, I moved to London and reconnected with Oscar.

Summer.

I think a woman in her 20s and 30's is in full bloom in her physical body. Everything is taut and gravity defying. Breasts, no matter their shape or size have that bounce and fullness that only breast cups or implants can give once this season of life passes. In summer, I grew to love my body and love sex, both thanks to Oscar. My love, I keep going back and forth about whether I would change this part of my story. What I should tell you and what I should take to my grave.

And even as I write this, I am thinking …they say experience is the best teacher. I say, sometimes. Experience is the best teacher, sometimes. I think other times, learning from the knowledge, wisdom and life lessons others have already learned the hard way is better. In my old age, I appreciate every experience I went through, but I do not want you to suffer in order to be wise, my Ruba. At least, I would rather you be informed and have the knowledge you need to make your own choices, which you will. You will choose the things that bring you love and joy, pain and sadness. Only you can live and lead your own life. My responsibility is just to inform you of what one set of choices looks like, just so you know and so you can choose more carefully. How I wish women would talk together more!

So here goes………………………………………

"Mamie!!"

"Huh"

"Time for your meds and bed love. You are falling asleep."

"Huh…Oscar…"

"Who? Mamie. It's me, Catherine. Wake up!"

"Huh! Yeah…all this writing is making me tired."

"You can finish tomorrow."

"You've got your coat on"

"Yes, I've usually left by now remember. I thought you'd have wanted to head to bed before 10:00 p.m. as usual but you seemed so into the letter, I didn't want to stop you. It's 11:00 p.m. I need to head home too. Here, take your meds and I'll lock up"

"Right. Ok. See you in the morning then."

~~~
~~~

Ruba, this letter is for you but it has me so energised! It is 6:00 a.m. and here I am, up and writing already. I am usually up by now. Drinking tea on the balcony as I watch the sunrise. Then I'd read the news on the app you gave me or watch TV. I am usually bored by 8:00 a.m., counting the minutes until Catherine gets here at 10:00 a.m. We do my bath and medications and then go out to our programs for the day. I'm not going anywhere today. I must finish this letter to you.

Last night, I dreamt of Oscar! It was so real. Oscar is that love at first sight, electric feeling that I think a woman can only ever experience once. In my case, it was love at second sight really, because I had spent my first few weeks in London with Oscar at the childminding program. Suzanna came to meet me at the train when I moved back to London. It was summer, 1948. I was going to stay with her family and save up, then move into a flat together and both start college. We were the children of post-war England. Suzanna was going to do Nursing; I was going to do Education and a Social Services certificate. I wanted to work with refugee children, abandoned children and all the newly immigrated qualified Blacks from the British colonies in Africa and the Caribbean pouring into post-war London to help with the labour shortages and rebuilding of the economy. I wanted to make sure children of these families got the education and support they needed to thrive as the backlash of racism was beginning to escalate. Our plans were on track, until the day we ran into Oscar on the tube.

That day, that moment, is one I will never forget. Even now, time stands still as I recall everything and everyone fading away except for Oscar and I. There we are, standing across from each other, hands barely touching again the stanchion pole that kept us from falling as the train swayed us forward. Suzanna was chatting, telling Oscar about how we had stayed in touch and all our plans, but my mouth was dry. Tongue-tied they call it. It's real you know. I felt limp. Every time I looked up, Oscar was staring right at me. I started breaking out in sweat, so I tuned in to listen to Suzanna. When I laughed, it was too loud in my ears. I didn't understand what was happening to me. Oh, my love, how I want you to experience this. Yet, I am not sure if I should tell you to run towards it or run away when it happens for you. I have lived long enough to know that sometimes, following this feeling bears good fruit and other times, it does not. I can give you no advice, other than to say watch the signals that tell you if it's amber or green and talk to the God of your father who I am starting to believe in, for guidance. That man will make me a Believer yet! But let me get to Oscar. You see, Oscar led me to you.

Three months after the train encounter, Suzanna, Oscar and I had been inseparable and I had moved out of Suzanna's to stay with him in his flat. Everyone tried to warn me. Aunty Nash, Suzanna, her parents. *You are moving too fast. What are his intentions? Will you still go to school? He is nice but doesn't seem to be doing much. His family is well-off, will they accept you?* I couldn't hear them. I had eyes and ears only for Oscar. He told me he would take care of me and we belonged to each other. I believed him. We first made love a month after the train encounter and then I can't remember a day after that that we didn't, except for when I had my period, Ruba! It seems like all we did was eat, sleep, have sex and occasionally meet up with Suzanna. I called him my Oscar Wilde. At first, he did not like it, mumbling about why I would liken him to an Irish gay guy. I ignored him. I've never been one to give attention to prejudice talk. Instead, I'd laugh and read him an Oscar Wilde quote or poem. Eventually, he started loving these readings and he stopped protesting when I called him my Oscar Wilde, especially after he drew something spectacular.

Even Mama Subi warned me about Oscar! We had been speaking occasionally over the years and then she finally came to London after the war, the year I turned 20. Oscar said it'll be better for me to reconnect with her on my own so he went off to his parents' cottage in Beaconsfield, Buckinghamshire. Said he had to be there for an Artist's festival anyway. Turns out he spent the week with his parents and the high-society girl who was always going to be his wife.

Why can't I meet him? Mama Subi asked.

I thought it was better to reconnect with you alone and he had to be at an artist's festival this week anyway, I replied. *Mamie Nafisa Boima! This will not bear good fruit. I did not leave you in London for this? What am I supposed to tell your dad of how you are doing? Please my child, my only child. Leave this boy and go back to school.*

In retrospect, I could see how he always managed to convince me things were my idea and always got out of me meeting his London-based friends or family. There was always some reasonable explanation.

I want to wait till we are ready to announce. I want to surprise them. I want it to be a grand engagement event.

The amber signs were already flashing but I was a fool in love. I believed him.

I attempted to start my program but I could not focus. After class, Oscar would be waiting for me and off we went. I would try to study and Oscar would doodle with his drawings for a while. But then he'd throw washable paint at me and next thing you know, we are making love on one of the giant canvases on the floor, painting it with our bodies. I had put away his drawing of me and had left it in my will to you, my love. But I shall take it out now and give it to you with this letter, then you will see a bit of what it was like for me to be seen by him and how I glowed at that moment in time. The look on my face, sultry, with lips pouting. The curves of my breasts and hips depicting my confidence in my chocolate skin and the height of my womanhood. We were in our bubble, until the day I confirmed I was pregnant.

Oscar screamed at me, red in the face. *How could you be so stupid! We can't have a baby! You have to figure it out 'aight mate. Figure it out!* I was numb. His reaction was hitting me like an avalanche. Cold, unexpected. He'd seen me take the daily pills; what did he mean how could *I* be so stupid? I could not process, so I just said I'm going for a walk, and left. I came back after 3 hours of walking aimlessness around and finding myself at a coffee shop with an empty tea cup that I don't remember buying or drinking. Oscar was gone. He left a note saying he would be at his parents' place for a month. He expected me to either be gone or to have dealt with things by then. He'd left a wade of money on the desk.

Heartbreak. Loss. That rite of passage through womanhood and life. The shadow that comes with love. One way or the other, my love, you will walk through this as long as you are alive. If not, because someone you love breaks your heart, it will be because you lose someone you love, just like you will lose me someday soon. Two weeks after Oscar left, I came to consciousness on the floor of the flat, wondering if I would ever get up again. My heart was broken in so many pieces, I was sure it would never heal and mend. Abandoned. Again. I discovered it was heart wrenchingly possible to lose oneself because of love. To no longer know who you are because of loss or to care nothing for your body or your life. I had spent the weeks agonizing over what to do, crying, walking around the flat wondering what was happening to my bubble. I felt used and too ashamed to call anyone after how I had behaved. I booked the abortion and was told someone had to go with me. Then just as I was gathering strength to call Suzanna, the bleeding started. I managed to get myself to the clinic.

Spontaneous abortion. You are miscarrying. Sorry. Nature will take its course. Come back for a check in a week, yeah?

I thought I'd be relieved, but instead, I was consumed by an empty coldness. Raw from the pain. Surprised by the shame I felt at my relief that I miscarried and the decision to abort taken out of my hands. Then, I was assailed by all these questions. How could I go back in shame and tell my mother she was right? How could I admit to my self-righteous arrogance that had made me think I was immune to the heartbreak Mama had warned me of? How could I have thought Mama was jealous and didn't want me to experience love because of the love she had given but not received in return? I heard the phone ringing and ignored it as I had for the past 2 weeks. I did not want to speak to Oscar. I got up to change my pads again when I could feel the blood seeping through my legs. I hadn't even been checking like the doctor had said to make sure I was passing all my clots. I think I would have been happy to sink into darkness and nothingness.

At some point, I realised the banging I was hearing wasn't in my head but from the door. I ignored it, thinking it was the mailman who would eventually leave a note and go away. Then I heard Suzanna's voice. Calling, screaming, threatening to call the police if I didn't open the door. I dragged myself to the door and opened it. Oscar's high-society engagement had made the tabloids and she had come looking for me right away. Suzanna tells me I was quite the sight. Nappy hair matted wild. Bloodied and food-stained pyjamas. Smelly and gaunt. She saved me. She cleaned me up. Stayed with me. Rocked me to sleep through my sobs. Then, she made sure we cleaned out of the flat before the month was up.

That was so early in my summer, My Ruba! I was only twenty-one by then and I became a dangerous woman. I went back to school and did degrees in education and counselling psychology. I used men for my pleasure, then walked away as soon as I felt a tinge of affection or they expressed anything more than lust or infatuation for me. I was not interested in love. This one guy drew me in more than anyone had since Oscar. His name was Frederick. London-born to Bajan parents who eventually left him with an aunt and uncle and returned to Barbados. We bonded over our shared heritage and sense of abandonment. Then I got pregnant. I had an abortion without telling him. Then I took a job in the farthest place where I'd been considering an offer. Yukon, Canada.

Autumn.

Suzanna who came to visit right away stood with me the night before my thirty-eight birthday and we witnessed our first midnight sun and summer solstice in Yukon together. When I think of Yukon, I think of coming of age. Of turning 40 and growing into my own. I was the farthest away from home and family, I've even been, but I loved this season of my womanhood the best. There is just something beautiful about the all-round maturity of that season. I think a woman's summer is marked with intensity, whereas autumn is marked with clarity. A sharper vision and focus. I thrived in my practice and enjoyed getting to know and work with the Indigenous Peoples of Yukon. I got referrals to many who were of both Indigenous and African heritage and as I journeyed with them, I healed too. I built my internal strength in those years.

I became more connected with family than ever before. Over the years, some of my siblings had also migrated abroad. We had in equal part, siblings who had stayed in Freetown or on the African continent as we had siblings who had migrated abroad. Some immigrated as students, others because they married someone who had immigrated and still others because of work relocations. At some point, we realised we had someone on every continent and decided to do bi-annual trips where we met at one siblings' country of residence. So it was that I spent my 40s and 50s visiting everywhere from Indonesia and Singapore to China, India, Jordan, Australia and New Zealand and even Iceland. Such a wonderful time in my life! But I am ahead of myself, because I need to tell you about my summer trip to London in '73.

I went to visit Aunt Nash and Mama Subi who had gone to London for some medical care. I decided to close my practice for the summer so I wouldn't have to rush back. They were both aging, so I wanted to spend time with them. They had carers, so I took them to appointments but also had time to visit and go out with old friends. It was clear they were good company for each other. They didn't really need me, but I felt obligated to do my duty and be there. That meant I could spend quite a lot of time with Suzanna too. She had married well as we said in those day and I enjoyed the company of her husband George, who for all his wealth was down-to-earth and clumsily funny. He was a lot like the characters played by Hugh Grant! I am so sorry you won't remember meeting them, but I'm glad you have picture evidence of them with you as a baby. That summer, we enjoyed the social season so much—Wimbledon season tickets, horse trials, Polo in the Park and I even got to go to the Royal Ascot as their guest. It is there I ran into Oscar and his wife.

We barely spoke. We said hello and shook hands rather formally. His wife was pleasant and chatty but I could feel a Yukon freeze coming out of every part of my body, directed at her. So, I offered a half smile in return to her pleasantries and walked away as politely as I could. I was both surprised and not, by the intensity of my physiological reaction. The counsellor in me knew what it was about. We had had no closure. I had tried to make my peace but had done so independent of Oscar and there I was, faced with him. Every part of me felt chilled to my bones, while my blood pressure simultaneously started going up at the visceral reminders of the pain he'd caused me. But my hand was tingling. The handshake was a mistake.

He appeared at my side, drink in hand. He slipped me a napkin under the guise of helping me wipe a spill. The napkin said: *Call me. I'm sorry for everything. I'd like to talk. Please don't throw this out.* There was a number scribbled hastily on the bottom. I went to throw it out, then stopped and put it in my handbag.

Suzanna begged me not to call him and not to go. I told her not to worry. I needed the closure too. We met, my Ruba. He started trying to explain and apologise. He said he had looked me up and knew I never had the child even though I had left when he got back to the flat. *You expected me to stay after you got engaged?* I asked. I told him to spare me. All I'd come for was closure. Our closure was having the wildest time in bed Ruba, just like I remembered it was like in our 20s. I had known all the while that it would happen. The hand tingle had warned me and I chose not to resist. I could tell by the way he looked at me at the Ascot he wanted me too. You will always know by the way a man looks at you Ruba, so pay attention and choose carefully who you say yes to. It could be the difference between one lustful encounter and a lifetime of emotional entanglement.

Oscar fell asleep right after, which men who have crazy sex like that in their 40s will do. I wiggled out of the bed and got dressed. I wrote him a note on the back-side of the napkin he'd given me:

"Always forgive your enemies; nothing annoys them so much." Oscar Wilde. P.S. All forgiven. Thank you for the closure. Have a great rest of your life.

I understand Oscar stalked Suzanna for a while because I wouldn't return his calls. Exactly nine months later, I had Mina at age forty-five. I did not tell Oscar. I spent the next fifteen years working and engrossed in raising and travelling with Mina to visit with my family and show her off.

Winter.

What can I tell you about a woman's winter? It is like the aurora borealis, the Northern Lights. Beautiful in retrospect and in the brilliance of what can be reborn from the ashes of life's lessons. The time when you look back and realise no tear has been wasted. Most women enter their winter having gone through menopause some time in their mid to late autumn. I was lucky that my transition was relatively straightforward, compared to what I hear from my friends. I had some hot flashes and became a lot more temperamental during my cycle than I ever was before. Thankfully, just when I thought I might need to consider my medication options, my body seemed to come into balance and my periods became less and less until they tapered off.

I wonder why it is called MENopause though. If I could influence a dictionary change, it would be called WomanTransform or something like that. You see, a woman's seasons marks her journey through the circle of life so much more clearly and starkly than a man's journey. Our winter might be marked by the end of our bodily reproductive functions, but it is the beginning of our transformation into the wisdom that only comes with advanced years of living life as a woman, whether one bore children of her own or not. Women in all circumstances raise villages and contribute to families in more ways than I can count! A woman in her 60s and beyond is simply a matriarch.

At 60, I moved to Vancouver. I preferred the more temperate weather at that stage. I had had enough of the long Whitehorse winters. There, Mina graduated high school and went to Simon Fraser University where she met your father, Morris. Their graduations, engagement and wedding were joyful days of this winter. It is such a time of acute awareness of the beauty of life because of the intensity of life in this season. Friends and family passing away have routinely reminded me of my mortality. It makes me grateful for each day I breath.

At the same time, I have watched your mother in her spring and summer and saw her making better choices that I ever did. Then there's your father Ruba, an out of this world guy. So handsome, faith-filled and responsible. I grew up with both the Muslim and Christian faiths, but I never paid attention to either. He is making me think, but maybe it is just because I am old now and might as well pay attention to otherworldly things. I've tried meditating and sometimes now I think I hear angels singing so my time may be drawing nigh. I was already old at 80 when you were born. The blessing of a baby girl, 10 years younger than her brother! By the time you were born, I had walked the journey of possible secondary infertility with Mina. It had been her Grandma's story and I encouraged her and bade her to care for your brother Malik and not abandon him in her pain like Mama Subi had done with me. Then, after all science had failed them, here you came. A wonderful, unexpected gift. A true blessing!

You need to know that it was after your birth I contacted your Grandpa Oscar. As age will do, I had softened, realizing that we were all about to die and I did not want to live a lie and let a legacy of pain carry forward. Suzanna found his number and I called. I told him I had a child for him after all and that he now had a grandchild. He wept. His wife had passed and they had never had a child. He came to see you and Mina a few times, then he upped and moved here without telling me!

The last five years of being with him as a companion and watching you and Mina bond with him and heal were the best times of my life. Redemptive. Healing. A fairy tale kind of story that doesn't happen every day. We may even have found forgiveness from God for all our infidelities these last few years after all the praying Morris has been doing here for generational healing over family meals! I still cannot believe that it was I who flew to England to bury Oscar and that Suzanna and I were standing at his graveside. Then I lost Suzanna a few short months after that. My heart has been so heavy this past year of loss! Thank God for you, Mina, Morris, Malik and Catherine, dear Catherine, whose friendship has sustained me through these pains! But I am 91, love…and it is only a matter of time before I join them.

~~~

It was almost 2:00 p.m. Mamie had stopped only to eat and take her medications when Catherine brought them to her.
~~~

"Mina said they will be here soon in the next hour or two. I have started reading *Eat, Pray, Love* while you've been typing. You're gonna love it!"

"Ok great. Thanks Catherine. I need a bath then before they get here, but first, can you please help me find something in the storage room? It's a rolled-up painting…"

An hour later, they had found the painting and Mamie had showered, eaten and taken her medications again. She was exhausted, but so satisfied. What a wonderful journey through memory lane the past 48 hours had been! She leaned into her lounge chair to rest and wait for her family to arrive. She was so so tired. She heard her own breathing turn rhythmic, laboured. Catherine was still chattering. She felt warmth. Like an envelope of love and gratitude embracing her. She was so ready. She smiled, as she drifted off…

9. ONCE UPON A TIME

I grimace.

> I didn't want to do it, but so many of you have and have posted about it so here goes. It is becoming the cool thing to do, so I did it too. But to me, it feels like a fad. A moot point. What difference does it really make? What does it really matter in the grand scheme of things? I have a great life. Wonderful friends and family and every reason to call myself blessed. Why raise the dead? Life is, what it is…we ARE moving on…

I am about to hit post. Then realise I am wiggling my fingers over the button instead. That's what I do when I am not sure about something. Wiggle my fingers and shake my left leg incessantly, as if the movement will shake out the thought that is making me feel uncertain. I save the post for later. Time to leave the office.

I pack up, throw my man-bag over my shoulder and start my walk to the elevator, Toronto Raptors Stealth Water Bottle in hand.

"We the North!" Khalid shouts out.

"We the North!" responses echo back.

I respond with a "woot woot," raising my bottle into the air. Three weeks after the historic NBA Finals win and the euphoria is anything but over. I am grinning by the time I get to the elevator. It was a great time to be alive in Toronto.

My phone is buzzing. I reach for it with a sigh. *Carol.* I look at the screen and sure enough her smiling image is bobbing up and down. Ever since I told her I prefer to talk before and after work because I get all consumed during the workday, she calls, exactly at 6:30 a.m. when I am heading out in the morning and exactly at 5:05 p.m., just as I am stepping out of the elevator. I consider not picking up, but then decide it isn't worth the constant ringing that would follow. *Besides, she has good reason today.* It is Friday night and it is Beza and Ahmed's *joint Bachelors and Bachelorettes night out:* "Hey Pretty..."

A few hours later we are out on the night. Laughing, dancing, carrying on. Beza and Ahmed's family and friends are all here and then there's us, the wedding party. Nick is drunk again and making a fool of himself, hitting on every girl who looks like she used a fake ID to get into the lounge. Nadia and Tolu are pretending not to care what each other is doing, while the rest of us know they will be back together again by the end of the night. Same old, same old. I hope they are together on the wedding day because it will make all our lives so much simpler. I keep trying to stop Carol from organizing everyone and making plans for the next weekend, the weekend after that, all the way to Caribana...

"Babe, Beza and Ahmed are going to need some downtime on their own you know."

"Pleaseeee! When you wait 7 years to get engaged and then are engaged for 18 months, what do you need time away like real newlyweds for?! We are not waiting that long, right bae?!"

I almost choke on my drink and make sure I'm distracted with mopping my shirt to avoid a direct response. Thankfully, the final member of the wedding party, Ayla walks in at that moment. We all shout various versions of Ayeeeee Ayeeeee!!! I sigh in relief. Ever since Beza and Ahmed got engaged, Carol has been laying the hints on strongly and regularly. I'm actually beginning to think about it. Only trouble is I am now wiggling my fingers over my drink and my left leg is shaking.

"What are you worrying about, bae?"

She knows me so well. She draws close and strokes my forehead as if to wipe away imaginary worry lines.

"Nothing. Nothing at all." I pull her close, rub her check the way she likes me to and give her a kiss.

We take a selfie at the end of the night. When I go to post it, my draft post from earlier is still on my screen. I delete it and post instead:

> This is what a happy wedding party celebrating Beza and Ahmed in the TO tonight looks like! We are splitting up from here. Let the bachelorette and bachelor party shenanigans begin!
> #AhmedBezaTown #WeddingTings

~~~

Somehow it is now Sunday morning and my phone is buzzing. I open my right eye, become conscious of a throbbing behind it and quickly close it again. The buzzing continues, as does the throbbing. My brain slowly registers two facts. It must be past 9:00 a.m. because my Do Not Disturb turns off at 8:59 a.m. on weekends...and that must be my parents calling! Their timing is as predictable as Carol's. I roll over fast and grab the phone just before it stops ringing to answer the WhatsApp video call. I tell myself this is why I never bring Carol or anyone else home on Saturday nights. The truth is, I just can't bring myself to. Somewhere in my brain and heart I believe that if I do, I would finally have failed my parents and myself.

"I was about to shout hallelujah! My son must have found his way back to church!"
~~~

"Hi Mom, Hi Pops"

"Hi sonny. How you doing?"

"Doing great Pops. How was preaching today?"

"Praise the Lord! We saw miracles today…"

I lean back and let the Baptist minister and his wife regale me with the miracles of the day. I offer the occasional "uh-huh, uh-huh." I have learned that if I keep them distracted enough talking about church and retired life in Jamaica, there's usually no time left to talk about me. I like it that way. It's funny that I feel like this, I muse, as they keep talking.

They have been pretty cool parents. Other than mom's hints that she would like me to go back to being a regular churchgoer, they didn't really insist on me doing things their way or any other way for that matter. They didn't say no when I wanted to join chess club or when swimming was my preferred sport. I grew up with mom taking me to the pool and cheering me on all the way through lifeguard training and competitive swimming. It was the same with my brother and my sister. We all played classical music. My brother played curling and my sister chose first to perform on cruise ships and then to travel with Cirque du Soleil over training to be an Olympic athlete. They say she was gifted enough to set new world records. Mom says she started doing acrobatics from the womb. Her reason for her choice was that she preferred to see the world. In the end, we all did things that were unusual for Black-Canadian kids of Jamaican descent. Our parents let us watch *Lord Have Mercy*, which not all churchgoing parents in the community were happy about. So, why do I always feel the need to hide?

My siblings acted the same way and we likewise hardly share what we are up to even with each other unless it comes up in conversation. Take my conversation with my sister Elizabeth yesterday. We are Irish twins, barely thirteen months apart. She casually told me she's finally tired of all the travel so she's taken a performance contract in Vegas.

“Oh,” I said. Did you tell the parents?”

“Why would I?” She answered.

And we spoke no further about it.

My brother seems happily married and enjoying his job—something in technology I don’t understand. He was always quiet and did his own thing. We never really spent time together since he was ten and eleven years older than us. I call on my niece and nephew’s birthdays and at Easter, Christmas and New Year’s. I only hear what he or his family are up to then.

My parents are still droning on. Mom is talking about all the things she’s up to with the women’s ministry and the local missions they are planning. I frown, then realise I am frowning at the image of Sister Hilary in my head. I shake my head to clear the image, then feel shame that I am still annoyed with Sister Hilary. She passed several years ago and here I am, still frowning and trying to shake off a dead woman. Then again, the memory of her has me thinking: *Maybe it wasn’t really them we were hiding from, but everyone and everything else. Maybe we just somehow learned to protect the freedoms we had with them by not letting them know all the other ways we chose to step outside the norm.*

I remember Sister Hilary and the ladies’ ministry team being at our house for brunch. It was one of those beautiful spring days that brings a glimpse of summer with it. We had just gone through the ritual of daylight savings time and the effect of changing our clocks by an hour was showing. The afternoon sunlight was lasting longer into the evening. The flowers were blooming. The air smelled fresh. It was warm enough to be outdoors and enjoy the clear blue skies and sunshine before the temperature cooled off in the early evening air. The ladies were still in their Sunday best, sitting on the porch, sipping ice tea in polka dot midi dresses, feathered hats and stockings. Sister Hilary was an usher and still had her gloves on too. To me, they all looked like clones. Elizabeth and I were fascinated with the hats. We were playing an irreverent guessing game about their hats from our vantage view of the lawn chairs in the yard, where we had been gifted cookie treats and lemonade as a fringe benefit of the brunch gathering.

We were just about bored enough and about to slink away quietly when we heard the ladies change their conversation from event planning to their children.
"My Jeffery just finished top of his class again and won another literary prize. We are praying for scholarships to the top American universities."

Elizabeth looked at me and rolled her eyes.

"To God be the Glory! My Chantal is getting straight A's still. How is George doing in track and field?"

"His times are improving! His coach is training him hard so he can make the Olympics trials."

I remember the pause and thinking it strange for them to be out of words when Sister Hilary piped up.

"First Lady Amber, will you not make Elizabeth train for the gymnastics Olympics instead of wasting time on theatre and the circus performances? I keep hearing how gifted she is. She must not waste her gifts! And Ebenezer, can he not join the others in track? He will never make it in swimming. You know our people can't swim! And as for curling…"

My mother had remained as cool as she always was and with a gracious smile had interrupted:

"Sister Hilary, thanks for the advice. You can call me Sister Amber like everyone else and my son prefers to be called Ben. Our children are doing what they love and that's all that matters to Daniel and I."

"But surely…you do know your call is to lead by example. This circus business is the way of the world, you know, it could lead to all sorts of things. And as an older woman I must admonish you to stop indulging them. And stop raising them to be white. They are black children."

"Sister Hilary, they are also Canadian children. We may be of Jamaican descent and I honour that, but Daniel's family has been here for five generations and were among the first businesses on King Street. Mine have been here for three generations. We were all born here. We are raising them to be all they can be. Now let's finish talking about the seating plan…"

On the way out as we helped pass the ladies their shawls and spring jackets, Sister Hilary bade me a pointed:

"Good day Ebenezer!"

I cringed and muttered back, "Good day." I really wanted to say F-off, but I knew that was one line my parents would not let me cross. Sister Sharon gave me a hug and said

"Thanks Ben, Keep up the good job with your swimming."

I liked Sister Sharon.

Dad is now saying:

"Remember Jeffrey? Well, his dad moved here y'know. Been the answer to his healing prayer all des years. His arthritis is so much better. We actually were shooting hoops again the other day, Lawdy Lawdy!! It was good times"

I enjoy listening to how much stronger their patois accents have become. I remember Jeffery's dad well. I loved it when Jeffery and I joined them and a few other father and son pairs to shoot hoops. He was a church elder and I remember he and my dad getting along and often talking about how to raise sons in a world that felt so confusing. A world in which being a man was beginning to mean different things than it meant when they were growing up. So they shot hoops and talked about raising sons. And raising black boys into black men.

Jeffery and I got closer during those years too and I remember that his dad's standard farewell to us when we were leaving his house was: "you boys stay safe now." And even though we lived only walking distance away, I remember that in a time when police encounters escalated among black and brown youth and carding was on the rise in the Greater Toronto area, Jeffery's dad would always walk me home as long as it was dusk. I remember that he would intentionally greet everyone along the way, black, brown, white with a "hello," "good day," and a nod and smile.

I loved watching Jeffery's dad. He felt larger than life. I felt safe with him. As I got older, I remember through teenage and young adulthood, only feeling that same sense of safety in public when I was with white friends. It was during those years that Jeffery and I and a lot of the kids I grew up with lost touch. That's one thing I'm thankful to social media for. I am 'friends' again with all the neighbourhood and church kids I grew up with. It's nice to feel connected and see how everyone is doing even if just superficially. And Jeffery and I run into each other and we are still friendly when we do. I might ping him today.

Mom's saying:

"How are things with you and Carol?"

That's my cue to end the call.

"We are doing good mom. Still dating. Everything is good with me. I have to head out to do errands soon so talk again next weekend."

"Ok Sonny. We need to call your sister now too. You checking on her?"

"Yeah, we spoke this week. Ok bye."

"Bye bye."

I hang up, turn off the phone and get ready to go back to sleep. Carol knows she's welcome after about 10:00 a.m. on Sundays. If she calls and I don't pick up, she'll come on over anyway. We will go out for brunch and get groceries and likely end up at the sports bar up the road. The sports world was certainly nursing the NBA finals hangover but slowly moving on to women's soccer world cup and

Wimbledon. I will get back home by 9:00 p.m. and prepare for another normal week at the office.

~~~

It is far from a normal week at the office. I have just told Carol the news. She is staring at me. Then she starts blinking as if some dust or sand had blown into her eyes. She says nothing so I keep talking.

"I wasn't expecting this. The company just made the announcement and by the time I got back to my desk, my manager was waiting to talk to me about it. Just think about the experience I will be gaining, travelling and working across Africa and the Middle East. It's a big government funded contract and a once in a lifetime opportunity"

"What about us?" Carol says finally.

"Us, we remain, babe. I'll come back regularly in the first year and we'll see what happens"

It turns out to be both the truth and a lie but the joke is on me. I feel bad for lying to Carol but even though I didn't think we were headed to 'us,' my work abroad trip saves us. I never come back that first year. And, it only takes a few weeks for me to find out two things about the expatriate life. It can both feed your soul and destroy it.

First the feeding part. I fall in love with being loved. I fall in love with feeling freer than I ever have before. I fall in love with being just another man, not a black man. When I step out of the plane at my first stop at Kotoko International Airport and am enveloped in a blanket of heat that I had never experienced before, I feel as if I'm floating in a dream. This is something I had never even considered or wanted, yet it feels like what I have always needed.

There are many other expats alighting from my flight and going through immigration. I start spotting passports and am intrigued with the different nationalities so I make a point of speaking to people—Indonesian, Chinese, Indian, Lebanese, another Canadian, Americans, an Australian. I ask people what brings them here:
~~~

"Company has operations here. It's my eleventh time on the continent. It's addictive man. Lovely place and people. Feels like second home now." Says the Australian.

"Oh, I'm from here!" says the Lebanese carrying a British passport. "born and bred. My family goes back and forth to the UK but we run textile businesses here." I get a similar answer from the Indian.

"Infrastructure project." Says the Chinese.

The American husband and wife team: "I'm a geologist and she's a travel blogger. We love ecotourism and we fit in a bit of work and learning exchange for both of us in any way we can on our trips."

And the other Canadian is also from Toronto, a third culture kid called Kwame, born to Ghanaian immigrants.

"Oh man! Nice to meet you, man! This is home, man! You know how it is over there, Tryna set up shop here and move over eventually. Here's my number. 'Sap me. I'll take you around!"

I don't think I really understand what he means by "you know how it is over there" but within days, I do. I realise I am walking with my back straighter than I had known was possible when you are simply affirmed by being and seeing your reflection all around you and having no intrinsic fear for your safety. I realise it when I get to the end of one of my busiest first days. I was taken around Accra to complete my work onboarding details—documentation, a visit to the Canadian embassy and scouting my work locations. It was a day filled with interactions with security and cops. Yet, I never once stop to check my gait or what I am doing whenever I see a cop like I was conditioned to do growing up. I feel like I did when Jeffrey's dad walked me home, except I do not need his shadow covering me anymore. I suddenly understand my friend Tolu and what had always intrigued and gnawed me about him—it was the confidence he had that I did not, born of this gift of just being.

That day, when I get back to the gated expat compound, I start rewriting the post I'd started months before, the night of Beza and Ahmed's pre-wedding parties. It feels like such a world away from where I am now.

> Yo, I started this post months ago and couldn't bring myself to post it. Back then, I was annoyed. I didn't see the point of trying to dig into the past. Now, I am here on Ghanaian soil, at my first African stop of five for the year and I am becoming woke to some things. It is early days, but let me share the experience I had today…First, what I've been meaning to post about is…

My phone starts buzzing. It is Kwame.

"Man, what you up to?"

"There's a party at The Compound."

"Well, it's Friday night in Accra, I got a whole itinerary for you. Live music at +233, a friend has reservations for us at skybar, there's lots to do, man. How about I pick you and we can party hop for a while and then end back at the Compound?"

"Sounds like a plan, man."

"Ok. I'm on the road already and not far from you. See you in a couple of minutes?"

"Done!"

I save the post and go freshen up.

It feeds my soul to be hanging out in Accra by day or by night and being loved for being a Canadian. It is the same at every African city from there on—Freetown, Lomé, Brazzaville, Gaborone, Tunis, Harare, Nairobi, Victoria—it didn't matter where. It amuses me that it is such a different experience than being at home in Canada. I realise that being Canadian means I am deemed neutral and friendly—not part of the current world and race politics associated with America and not deemed as part of the European colonial history on the continent. The British association to Canada was not part of the consciousness or conversations here. Being a Canadian abroad was a win all around.

It also feeds my soul that black folks would quickly remind me that though I identify as Canadian-Jamaican, I am a brother, simply because of the widespread philosophy that "as long as you're a black man, you're an African." I love being taught by Kwame and others the ropes—how to avoid being charged foreign fees or scammed at the local market, when to tip and when to use foreign status to avoid giving a questionable fee for service (aka, bribe). And it also feeds my soul to be treated with dignity and status. Here, I am Mr. Ben to all, from the gateman at the Compound to the home and office staff assigned to me. I wake up to cooked meals, ironed clothes and washed cars. It is a life I never imagined back in Ajax.

I remain in love with all that I am seeing and learning. I only have to look around to be confronted with extreme wealth and extreme struggle, a plethora of opportunity and a sea of ingenuity. I marvel that in the places of daily struggle that I could never even imagine in spite of the social conditioning black people are subjected to around the world and back home, unbridled joy could always be found here. I am in sensory overload daily.

While I savour my soul-feeding experiences, I go through Freetown and a few more urban cities and rural African towns before I begin admitting the soul destruction slowly creeping over me. I notice how I feel superior and godlike. I exist in a cocoon, along with all the expatriates and foreigners. I am two-faced. A brother outside the Compound, a comrade inside. I smile, laugh and sometimes contribute to the stories:

"Can you believe the cop tried to scam me?"

"I've noticed money missing so I've been leaving little things I don't mind losing around and I am sure the maid has been stealing. These people never change—even after I paid school for her children!"

"The pompous idiot was trying to school me about the evils of multinationals and foreigners and the destruction we are causing. I've worked here for 25 years! I've helped and saved more locals than he ever has. Meanwhile, he's fully western-educated, complete with a Harvard degree of course!"

When it becomes too hard for me to nod along, I tune out, collude with my silence and light a cigar. That's the newest habit I have picked up. I realise that I am so used to blending in, I don't know how to speak up without becoming the image of the militant black man I have always avoided.

I take advantage of being foreign to bypass line-ups and take reservations that should have gone to my local brothers and sisters waiting outside. I am quick to criticise local practices I don't understand but adopt those that endorse my brotherliness. And I begin to join in on the revelry of elevated expat status to wine and dine the women who so much as smile at me at lunch time.

It is in Harare as I have dinner with Rose and we share a shisha tank with other single expats and their local dates that I realise how far gone I am. I notice that I am in the midst of the never married, recently broken-up or divorced singles who have arrived at the life that was more than they ever dreamed up and intend to live it up for the foreseeable future. I think of the people I admire for the various services and endeavours they are up to and none of them are where I am. One couple is on a service trip to the interior which they never publicise, they just do it. Another young woman who is making more headway than most organisations in facilitating local networks and real capacity-building joined us earlier but left after dinner and a few drinks. My idols were living and enjoying the expat life while upholding their values and doing great work. I was admiring them from afar, while getting drunk on the power that social freedom and status suddenly afforded me. I'd even been avoiding calls from my parents, Elizabeth and Carol.

I take Rose home and do with her as I had intended. I feel a pang of guilt as I offer her too much cash to buy herself a gift and phone credit so she can call me. She feigns surprise at my offer. I insist and she graciously accepts. A necessary ritual to absolve my guilt and fool her conscience. I call a driver to take her home. He later tells me she asked him to take her back to The Place. I'm glad I never compromise on condom use. I try to think of all the girls I've been with and they all blur. The one I dated for a while in Freetown, I liked a lot, but just couldn't shake the feeling she was with me for my foreign credentials and passport. I suddenly miss Carol's predictability and for the first time, I don't start wiggling my fingers or shaking my left leg when I think of her.

I call Carol but don't reach her. She calls me back later. Our pleasantries are strained at first. I am thankful she doesn't ask where I've been or why I stopped answering her calls regularly since Freetown. I know she knows. She's updating me on our friends.

"Beza and Ahmed are pregnant again. Number 3's on the way."

"Oh, and Tolu and Nadia finally broke up."

"Yeah right!"

"No, for real. She's pregnant and getting engaged this weekend to this other African guy who just moved here 6 months ago. I've never seen Tolu so devastated"

"What?! And babe, you can't say 'African guy.' What country is he from?"

"French African somewhere. Can't remember if it's Gambia, Senegal or Ivory Coast. Damn good looking and his name is Omari."

"Babe, Gambia isn't French Africa."

"Spare me the lecture."

"I love you."

"You must be missing home. It's late now, I gatta go."

It takes another month of talking daily before she loosens up again. I ask if she would come visit and at first, she says no. Another month later she finally agrees. It's getting close to my second Christmas away and this time, I don't want to be alone. She arrives the week before Christmas for a month. I ask her to marry me on Christmas Eve and On New Year's Eve, we get married at Victoria Falls. When I go back to Toronto in March for the first time since I left, my parents come to town and we have a blessing and a big cook-out and party in the old neighbourhood. And of course, my old man and his first lady preside.

~~~

"Happy Anniversary Grandpa Ben!"

Naomi, the new light of my life bounds in, hops straight on my lap and wraps her arms around my neck. Her thick and big curls tickle me under my chin. I like it, so I give her a squeeze and rub the side of my face again her hair and breath in coconut oil. It reminds me of Carol and I smile.

This is my happy place now. Naomi on my lap. Elizabeth across from me reading another self-care book. We've become inseparable in our old age, finally bonding after all the time we spent apart. You could say our new bond has been forged out of necessity. The need for companionship. Elizabeth never married and never had children. She says she never thought marriage or children were right for her or would fit with her lifestyle. She chose never to adopt either. Instead, once she moved to Vegas, she spent time volunteering at different youth programs and teaching gymnastics, acrobatics and contortionist skills. She opened a youth music and
~~~

performance studio when she eventually moved back to Toronto. We are 75 and 76 and she looks amazing. The years of physical fitness and performing have served her well. She looks no older than 50. I like to think I do too.

As for me, life with Carol was exactly what I had needed. She was just the piece of home I needed to be complete. She was my ally. My true soulmate. She made all the details of our lives abroad work. From ironing out ongoing employment contract details, to the community and non-profit work we became engaged in wherever we went, to our social calendar. I don't know how she did it all while landing teaching jobs everywhere and raising our twin sons.

It was Carol who pointed out my hypocrisies and inconsistencies, gently, yet clearly enough that I, in turn, learned to do so in our bubbled expat communities. It was Carol who pointed out that I spent Sunday mornings watching the people stream to church in their flamboyant feathered hats, just like my Ma and her Caribbean-descent Canadian friends. One day, she said: "We should join them one of these days, you know." So we did and I finally found my way back to Church. It was she who realised what I was afraid to say—that I couldn't imagine going back to Toronto. She orchestrated our lives so we stayed abroad, yet managed to come home to Toronto to see family and friends regularly and visit Jamaica to share our children with my parents before they passed away too.

A year ago, we were preparing to retire and thinking about where on the African continent we wanted to spend our latter years. In the meantime, we came home to Toronto as usual in the summer and did our routine medical tests. All was well. The next week, Carol complained of headaches and dizziness. She woke up one morning and headed to the bathroom. I heard her scream and heard a thud.

911.

Ambulance.

Flashing lights.

Emergency.

Scans.

"I'm sorry."

"We lost her."

"Brain aneurysm. Ruptured."

I have never felt as adrift as I did in the weeks and months that followed. I seemed to be losing my will to live. Our sons Nicholas and Nathaniel tried to console me the best they could. Nat, Naomi's dad had moved to Toronto to attend Queens University and met his wife and they helped me with all the appointments, paperwork and funeral planning. Nic had come over and was trying to stay as long as he could. He had stayed on the continent, attending the Pan African University and was working and teaching at the same institution which was ranked the #1 Global Learning University. I don't even understand how universities operate anymore. I love hearing Nic's stories of how they operate their virtual and satellite campuses and all the beam technologies making it possible, but it really makes no sense to me.

When Nic left, I took a further downturn. Depressed and lethargic. Then Elizabeth came over one day and told me we were going for a drive. Ten short minutes later, we were at the beautiful new complexes in development on the corner, looking at a duplex home. It was ours if I agreed, she said. I could retire and take my settlement. I could help her run the studio she had bought in the complex and teach whatever I wanted to. It was a diverse neighbourhood being tagged as an international village. My life experience would be marketable there. I joined Elizabeth and it saved me. I could no longer imagine living on the African continent without Carol.

I still miss Carol terribly but then here is Naomi, looking just like her, full of joy and inquisition. She loves puzzles and we are working on a 100-piece one. I can see us graduating to a 1000-piece puzzle soon. I have just finished regaling her yet again with the story of my Christmas and New Year's engagement and wedding at the beautiful Lake Victoria. I promise again to take her there soon if her parents agree to it. She pipes us:

"Grandpa?"

"Yes Naomi"

"How should I respond when people ask me where I am from?"

I straighten out and look at her. She continues: "I mean, I know we are from here in Toronto and so was Grandma. And your parents, parents, parents were from Jamaica but if all black people come from Africa, which country are we from?"

Elizabeth looks up from her book and say "oooohhhhhh, I wanna hear this too, Grandpa!"

I hesitate for only half a sec, then feel a sense of peace.

"Well, Your Granty over there doesn't know this but I do happen to know. A long time ago, I took a DNA test when it was the thing to do."

"WHAT?!" exclaimed Elizabeth. She is wide-eyed and her mouth agape.

"What is a DNA test Grampa Ben?"

"It's a test that tells you your genetic code. Imagine like computer codes and imagine that people who are related have a set of codes that do not change over generations. That's the DNA. It's like an identity code written into the cells that make up your body."

"Just spill Ben! How could you have known all this time and not said anything?!" Elizabeth's voice is high-pitched in anticipation.

"I'm sorry sis. We just never used to talk about these things…and then well, well, I kept meaning to post about it but never felt right because at first, I thought it wasn't important. I just did it because guys in the neighbourhood were and talked me into it. Remember Beza and Ahmed? I found out the week of their wedding. Then after the intensity of the culture shock and integration from living on the continent settled for me…I kinda forgot about it…"

"So where are we from?!" Elizabeth yelled.

"Our DNA was traced to 4 places overall. Our paternal ethnicity estimate is 70% Sierra Leonean (Mende) and 30% European (England and some Germanic). Our maternal profile is 67% Ghanaian (Ashanti), 18% Indian, 5 % Chinese and 10% North African and Arabian."

"What?! So we are from the world, Grandpa?!" Naomi squealed.

"Yes Naomi, we are mostly from Africa, but we are from the world."

"Wait What?! Wow! The testing is so much more advanced though, I wonder what it'll say now." Elizabeth quipped.

"We can find out." I said. "Otto! Get DNA samples and run our test sequences."

"Yes Mr. Ben. On it now. Results will be ready in 10 minutes"

"So how did us Africans come to be here, and be from Canada too?" Naomi asked.

I sigh: "Well, once upon a time…"

10. WE HUMANS, LOVE

The pilot noted she was flying over the perfect aerial spot to see the all-round beauty of the terrain and capture shots from their drone cameras. Dr Brown had been too busy scanning the statistics and updates coming into her glasses' monitor to pay attention to anything else. She took a breath and switched to look through the magnifier on her screen. She could see everything in sharp focus and zoom miles out in every direction. It was breath taking. Brilliant blues and greens of the North Atlantic and Mediterranean seas. The white-yellow beach banks and the yellow-red-browns of the Saharan sand dunes. The distinctive tops of majestic mountain peaks amidst dense forest vegetation and tall palm trees waving in the wind like flags to greet the viewer. The slopes swept into plateaus and valleys covered in lush tropical vegetation in some areas and desert views in others. It was all the beauty of African geography in one scene. They were headed to their debrief site nestled in an oasis spot in the deserts of Morocco.

She droned over to get aerial shots of the iconic Marrakech Menara Airport. She loved looking at the diamond halos it casts under its waved roof and she caught a shadow scene of them. The architectural and cultural marvel it represented symbolised what they needed to accomplish today. She took shots of it to share with her teams. It was a brilliant fusion of worldviews where cultures meet and exponentially beautiful outcomes are possible. East and West. North and South. Modern and Traditional. Old and New. Culture and Technology. She heard herself sigh and breathed again to stop her nerves fraying in the face of the enormous task ahead. *This is what's at stake. Our world.*

She snapped off her glasses and recalled gazing at the early rising sun just before they took off. She made a point of doing that often. Seeing with her naked eyes, feeling textures with her bare hands and inhaling the aromas of flowers against her nostrils. In a world of augmented reality, she found balance in staying grounded as much to the real as to the possible. She liked living in the space between. The sun had cast a brilliant red-golden hue over everything. There was nothing, absolutely nothing, like taking in the aura of a sunrise with the naked eye.

An hour later, Dr Brown alighted from the jet with her braids flowing behind her and hurried over to the briefing room where her technical team was ready and waiting for her. The head of the team handed her the e-clipboard and she flipped her glasses to the top of her head where they perched crookedly while she reviewed the data.

"Your group of ten, Ma'am."

"How are they doing?"

"They seem fine. Still shell shocked though."

"Understandable. We expected that."

She put the E-Headset on and entered their experiences, checked heart rates, pulses, mental states. They were all in good shape.

"How are the other sites doing?" she asked

"The results are astounding on every continent. Empathy and Acceptance are up globally. Reparations and genuine apologies are being made. Everyone wants to know what is making the leaders who were part of this make decisions they had refused to before. We have asked them to stop all communication, decision-making or actions now until after the debriefs. We have wait lists on every continent for the next intake."

"And the people still at risk of lasting harm?"

"The percentage is lower than we expected. The algorithms predicted 10% will break. The global total is 5%. The last report shows 3% are fully rehabilitated and recovered without the need for the memory wipe routine and reset of their pre-experiment states. We are working on the final 2% and hopeful they will recover normally so all can retain memory of the experience as well as the beneficial outcomes."

She wanted to weep with relief and felt overwhelmed at the same time. The gravity of what was happening hit her and she took a step back. She, just a little black girl who could, from Freetown, Sierra Leone had led this. What if it fails? What if the effects fade off like everything else?

She shook her head.

She couldn't allow fear to win.

There was still the debrief to be completed and a new creed to be created before this group could be released according to the plan. They had trained for this—scientists, social psychologists, groups therapists, sociologists, counsellors, educators. She should be ready, but she could feel bile rising with the panic circling up from her belly like a cyclone. The predictive analysis had shown that all the positive effects of the most daring human experiment in history could fall apart here, at this juncture. This was our human kryptonite. Making a decision for the good of all.

Today, would be the make or break proof of whether people could transcend their differences. If any of the debriefs on any continent went to impasse, the bet was off and there were those waiting in the wings to start modifying humans into robotoids, by removing all our emotional capacities. Rationality only will prevail. It would be the end of emotions of all kind—love and joy, anger and sadness and everything in between. We would register physiological responses simply as data.

She couldn't believe they had pulled it off. The proposal was risky at best, but their consortium of human sciences professionals could not let humanity be diminished and the Rationalists proposal stand. She could not believe when the Human Consortium chose her to be their spokesperson. Their argument was that yes, our emotions bring out the worst in us, but they also bring out the best in us. What would our world be like without love and joy even if we rid ourselves of anger and hate? The issue in human history has never been emotional reactions, it has always been decisions that are used to oppress and suppress. What would the world be like if we truly learned from our worst failings? What would the world be like if we acknowledge and process our emotions, then redirect them towards what is good and right? What would it be like if we are able to truly remember the pain of our past, lock into empathy and make decisions for the good of all?

She had made the proposal at the Assembly of every peace, development and international cooperation body known to man. Rather than use our advanced technology to numb, how about using it to truly lock into our capacity for empathy and learning, she proposed. What if people the world over who remain neutral or blind to others' sufferings could enter into those experiences and then decide on a new design for our world? People would be asked to sign-up, by voluntary consent. They will know that they will be put into conditions of sufferings that had actually occurred in the world, then asked to decide on policies and agreements for changing those conditions. The hurdle was whether people would actually say yes to this. Then she told her war survival story. How she can still smell decaying human flesh in her nostrils when she closes her eyes. How fireworks frighten her. How terror dreams of war wake her up often in the dark of night. When the voting started, she expected a slim win at best. She did not expect the landslide win that it was. The intake of people for the experiments was the next indication that the world was ready. The era of survival shows and *Hunger Games* had prepared the world for such an experiment. The recruitment started and the intake quota was filled globally in 48 hours.

She looked around at the expectant faces staring back at her in the strategy room. The hope on their faces helped her collect herself and muster her strength. She took her glasses off her head and put them down. She straightened out her Ankara African print lab coat. She muttered mostly to herself, "here goes," then tapped and entered straight through the translucent wall into the caucus room to meet her volunteers.

A hush fell on the room when she walked in.

"Ladies and Gentlemen…thank you." She had choked up at the sight of them.

They were the picture of survivors anywhere in the world, in every sense of the word.

Tattered clothing and emotions, but face forward.

Broken but far from destroyed.

Exhausted but triumphant.

Shocked yet determined.

Raw from the hurt and alive with possibility.

Survivors.

She had done enough post trauma counselling to know the ones who would overcome. And she was looking at them. She had the right group for the job.

A few of them choked up too, then furiously wiped the tears from their eyes with the back of their hands. The motion that says they mean business. There's no time for crying.

"When you joined this effort, you knew you were signing up for the greatest human experiment of all time. I can tell you that in our current tracking of outcomes, the whole operation was a success and worth the risks, but that's why I am here, so I can hear from you whether it was worth it and so we can complete our final task. We are to decide on a Creed for the world that holds governments, leaders, policy-makers and everyday people to always choose decisions for the good of all. A new world system, to be programmed into our central world code. Each debrief site is taking on a different task. Some must decide on climate change agreements, others on decisions to end inequalities, others stopping wars. We must all succeed in our decisions today for all of us to win. If we fail, we hand over the next phase of global decision-making to the Rationalists." They looked sombre and yet their faces radiated with conviction. They were ready for the challenge.

"First though, let's introduce ourselves. You were all at different global experiment sites focused on African and black concerns and global race relations so please introduce yourselves, tell us which simulation you were in and tell us why you joined the effort. You have all heard my story when you arrived and watched the recording of my speech at the Assembly." There were nods around the room.

"We are on African soil, so we will do this in the style of Elder Gatherings, modified to today's times. Please take her seat around the circle in front of your intergalactic web station. At any time during our sessions, you can put on your glasses to link in and see what is happening at the other debrief sites' deliberations. You can ask your personal MyRobot to get you any information, data or pictures you want. You can enter others' experiences to empathise with where they are coming from with your attached E-headset. At the end of our deliberations, you will each register your vote, your rationale and your emotional state. The WeRobot will run the algorithms and help us draw our final conclusions. WeRobot will also let us know if we have any byes or last chance alternative choices we can consider before we confirm our final agreement. That, ladies and gentlemen, will decide the fate of our world for the foreseeable future."

They stood frozen for what seemed like several minutes but was probably seconds. Dr Brown stepped forward and took her seat and one by one, they followed. When they were all seated, she motioned to her right and the first person started:

"My name is Hawa. I was born to middle-class Sierra Leonean parents' who were both international law experts and university professors. I lived in England, America, Portugal, Greece, Geneva and Singapore. I went to MIT and have spent time researching all the technology innovations coming from all over Africa. What can I say? I grew up privileged. African and Black stereotypes did not always apply to me. At the same time, I wanted to be responsible, not dismissive of the continued oppressions on the continent and elsewhere. I was in the simulation as a rural Liberian girl who crosses the border to Sierra Leone and is adopted by a family there, only to be caught in the war conditions that families in Kono experienced when rebels occupied the mining areas. Think the movie Blood Diamonds. In the simulation, I live in the forest for a month hiding from rebels with other children and experience losing all the others…"

"Hello. My name is Mahmoud. I was in the simulation of conditions faced by Black Sudanese peoples from Darfur and South Sudan. It was…beyond torture. I joined because I am fourth generation Lebanese decent, born and raised in West Africa. I grew up between Sierra Leone, Ghana and England. I joined because I am of Africa, but have been sheltered from her oppressions by the privileges and access to her wealth that I have had. But outside Africa, I have faced racism because I am seen first and foremost as Arab and profiled in all the ways 9/11 and terrorism in our world have created…"

"My name is Darell. I was in the simulation in the South African township experiences during apartheid. I joined the effort because I am African-America but it was my parents who went through the civil rights era, not me. I went to Yale and have struggled with black community saying I'm white washed, Africans and Caribbeans seeing me as 'Afro' and white community seeing me as black. Oh, and my grandmother was white. I joined because I just want all the craziness to stop…and then the apartheid experience…well…it was kind of familiar when I went through the simulated police arrest, but I could never have imagined the pain…."

"Waa Gwan. My name is Sue. Me ar Jamaican via Guyana. Me dad im Afro-Guyanese. Me just wan fit in dis worl, mon! Me open me mouth and all man confuse! Me go ah British Columbia simulation inna Canada fi experience how de imported Chinese work on de railroads with other black folks and native folks also. Lord have mercy! After the simulation, me feel dem ar indentured slaves not workers. Indentured slaves, me ah tell you! ..."

"My name is Jas. I am an Indo-Canadian born to Indo-Ugandan parents whose parents were exiled from Uganda under Idi Amin. I grew up with them always carrying on and acting homesick for 'Africa.' I was happy to be Canadian. When I took a gap year to work and volunteer in East Africa, I finally understood. It was great to be Indian in East Africa. All my relatives were much more well off than we were in Canada, but I realised quickly that locals didn't like me and my kind and no one accepted me as Canadian. They all wanted to know if I was from Pakistan, or India or somewhere like that. Never been to any of those places just like I'd never been to Uganda, Kenya or Tanzania until last summer. So, I did the Idi Amin era simulation. I wish I'd chosen something else…"

"My name is Andrei. In case you haven't noticed. I'm white, but I'm from Romania so I feel not always treated with the white privilege I hear about. I have an African wife from Niger. My son was beaten at school once and I almost lose my mind. When I go to restaurants with my wife, they always give me bill but she makes more money than me! She's a dentist! I'm Engineer and immigrant too. I think this is crazy! Then at work they do seminar on racism and microaggression and they tell me and my American friend here Robert that we are privileged and nobody listens to how we feel. I wanted to join to understand why nobody listens my side and I want my children and wife to have same respect as me. We joined slavery simulation where we the slaves! I understand now why no one listens…"

"I'm the other white guy, Robert. Whiter than white, with all the privileges. Southern, Christian background and all. I'm not gonna lie, I hated all the privilege talk and how it made me feel so guilty and ashamed and takes away all my status. Then I try being an ally and everyone just says sit down and shut up! Don't say Ma Nigger or My Main Man. I'm not even allowed to talk before someone says I put my foot in my mouth. I just want it all to fucking stop! ...that simulation though…I mean, I've watched enough of the American slave movies but simulating that experience, with the tables turned and the illusion that it was never-ending…I'm still scarred man. We gotta get this fixed right!"

"Hello, I'm Kim. I'm a white woman born in the Gambia and Africa is in my bones. I manage to integrate into African communities wherever I go and I have always been welcomed and accepted. I wear Africana outfits at community events and nothing gives me more joy than dancing with my African brothers and sisters. It's been hard for me to admit that even though I identify as African, I can hide behind the colour line. No one ever assumes I am from Africa unless I bring it up and I have been with my black sisters when they are asked ridiculous questions. One time, a friend of mine was asked what it's like to have a backside as big as hers and if it is heavy! He might as well have called her a Hottentot Venus! Yes, black people call me white woman on the continent all the time, but I was never excluded or mistreated because of it. In fact, I was just as privileged there as here. So, I joined the simulation for going through consistent microaggression with a release of the chemical that gave me the mental pain of that kind of social trauma each time. I am still trying to wrap my head around it…"

"I'm Halima. I wear hijab so you know who I am. My mother is from Northern Nigeria and was abducted before the Chibok girls. She had me in captivity. I don't know my father. I have always been angry because of that. So yeah, I joined the simulation on the Boko Haram practices." She was shaking her head from side to side, rubbing her temples and closed her eyes. "I just want it to stop. It's got to stop."

"I am Christian. I am an African man from Cameroon and I am gay. It is easier to live in France, but not so much among the African immigrant communities so I hang out with Third Culture African Francophones only, and white friends I grew up with since moving there as a child. I am not out as gay when I go home to Cameroon. Binyavanga Wainaina is my hero but I do not yet have the courage to live as he did. May his soul rest in peace. And may the simulation I just experienced of violence against those living out or found out as gay end forever by the time we leave this room."

There had been tears throughout their telling. Set jaws. Nervous ticks. A few had put on their glasses and transported themselves to happy childhood memories, favourite places or intergalactic images that helped them feel peaceful. Dr Brown monitored them throughout to make sure they could continue without breaking while everyone introduced themselves.

"Let's break for 30 minutes now. Take time to refresh yourselves and talk to each other further. When we come back, we go straight into deliberating what our global decision-making creed must say."

The deliberations started off well. Fuelled by their shared experiences and empathy. As they progressed, the triggers started.

"We need a fresh start. No more revisiting the past!"

"Easy for you to say! You should have been in my simulation!"

"I have known oppression too! I grew up poor and made it out by hard work!"

"Did you work on the railroads?"

"You people just don't understand!"

"We are so flawed. We will never learn! We should try being Robotoids. The Rationalists are right. That may be our only hope!"

Dr Brown let the dissent voices rise and knew just when to stop the deliberations before they got too escalated beyond repair. Her MyRobot and tracking of their physiological states helped her make the call at just the right time. They took another break, and when they came back, she could tell they were weary. She decided to call in the global statistics early and remind them of the stakes.

"WeRobot, please report" She said. Her heart was pumping so loud it could burst out of her chest.

WeRobot reporting: All sites are at impasse. The probability of mission failure is 99.9%.

A poignant silence fell over the group. Their physiological states registered flat lines. Defeat. Deadness. Surrender. There were no tears. They were beyond that. Yet as they stood immobilised the emotional state register started flickering a slim line of hope.

WeRobot also reporting there is one striking piece of data. In the 0.01% probability for success remaining, there is a consistent emotional state that makes the millions of associated cases successful. In every single one, the people who make positive decisions indicate an act of human love preceded their response. Here are the prototypic images with African or black context"

Their screens flashed with images and news clips. A black man saved a white child from drowning—the child's father was the cop who arrested him on a drug possession charge that turned out to be a plant. African children teaching students around the world about African geography and diversity via AugmentedReality headsets. White neighbours with black and brown ones having regular meals together. And on it went.

"So, in other words…" Dr Brown stated

"If we remove all capacity for love…" another continued

"We remove all chance that humanity will ever transcend differences and make decisions for the good of all!" another ended.

WeRobot reporting that is correct. In this scenario in which you humans put love above all from here on, my predictions show that this generation goes down in history as the ancestors who healed the world. You will be called the ReGenesis Generation.

"Wow! One of them." Exclaimed "So what are we waiting for?"

WeRobot reporting, I'm also showing that all sites are hedging to see who will first hit their Central Buzzer showing success. The probability of others following in the same direction increases as soon as one site enters success or failure

The room went still. All looked around at each other.

Dr Brown stepped forward. Let's start our Creed with this

then:

We Humans, today commit to put love over all, in all scenarios…

They ended the Creed with the short form declaration statement:

We Humans, Love.

They hit the Central Buzzer. It was silent for 5 minutes that felt like eternity. They were all escalated with anxiety.

Then one failure button came in.

Followed by success. Then another success, after success outcome.

When 51 teams around the world had entered success, they flung off their glasses' and started screaming for joy, laughing, crying and chanting:

We Humans, Love!

We Humans, Love!

We Humans, Love!

Dr Brown could not wipe the grin off her face with her tears as she stepped away from the celebrating group. She tapped through the wall back into the logistics room. There was still much coordination to complete to spread the success of this and set-up the next intake. She was certain of one thing more than ever before.

When We Humans Love,

Love. Wins.

Lonta. Na De Wod Dat. The End. Word!

ABOUT THE AUTHOR

Dr Yabome Gilpin-Jackson considers herself a dreamer, doer and storyteller, committed to imagining and leading the futures we want. She is an applied social scientist, working in the areas of human development & leadership/organization development as a scholar, consultant, writer. She is a proud African-Canadian who was born in Germany, grew up in Sierra Leone, and completed her studies in Canada and the United States. Among other awards, Yabome has been named International African Woman of the Year by UK-based Women4Africa and was the first ever recipient of the Organization Development Network's Emerging Organization Development Practitioner award in the United States. She has also received the prestigious Harry Jerome Professional Excellence Award in Canada.

Dr Gilpin-Jackson has published books, chapters and peer-reviewed journal articles in her fields. Yabome continues to research, write and speak on leadership & organization development issues, posttraumatic growth & on honouring diversity and social equality in our locally global world. She is the author of Identities, a short story collection about global African experiences. She is also initiator, co-founder and lead editor of We Will Lead Africa, a non-fiction anthology of everyday African leadership stories. Yabome is community-engaged on various Boards, including Canadian-based NGO, The People's Foundation for Sierra Leone & The Mayor's Advisory Board for Black History Month in Vancouver.

Quote: ***"The core of my work, in relation to Africa, is the desire to tell more wholesome narratives of African identity and leadership experiences on and off the continent, that go beyond existing stereotypes and assumptions."***

You can find Dr Gilpin-Jackson online at:
www.SLDConsulting.org; Twitter: @supportdevelop
Facebook: @yabomewriter; Amazon:
https://www.amazon.com/author/yabomegilpin-jackson;
Linkedin: https://www.linkedin.com/in/yabome/

NOTE FROM YABOME ON WHY THIS PROJECT

This collection of stories came from the realization that identities and belonging are two sides of the same coin; intertwined into our human need to be and live fully as an individual AND in community. Who we are and how we identify, will dictate the communities and spaces where we can find belonging. Each one of us must form/transform our sense of identity and belonging in order to bring our best to the world. We do this, through our own stories and narratives about who we are and how we fit, or do not, into society. We shape our worlds by our stories.

However, in order to belong, to integrate into the world around us, each of us must self-differentiate, a natural part of our human development. I must get clear who I am. The process of becoming an individual. Then, and only then, can I choose where I belong in society. This isn't always a simple process because of two reasons. First, where cultural norms we are born into assume on behalf of individuals, who they are, and second, where the society at large further classifies a social hierarchy of dominant groups and others. Global Africans, especially 'black' Africans, face both challenges.

Global Africans are that community of peoples born on or off the continent who live a significant part of their lives in global spaces.
From an identity perspective, African cultures have broadly been described as a sociogenic worldview by African developmental psychologist, A. Bame Nsamenang. This worldview assumes individuation depends on enacting social roles and communal responsibilities as central to selfhood. This is most commonly framed and best described in the popularised Ubuntu description of this philosophy from southern Africa—I am because you/we are. This continues to apply to global Africans who must then live between this sociogenic world and the global cultures they also inhabit.

From a belonging perspective, the social status of 'other' means global Africans are often struggling for belonging—both because of historical realities that have stripped cultural artefacts and anchors of belonging from global Africans and because of ongoing narrow views and narratives of what it means to be an African. This means global Africans will often find themselves underrepresented in mainstream spaces. They must both find their own ways of receiving support and validation and negotiate how they integrate into society. It is a complex and delicate dance to be in this liminal space between worlds.

Ancestries builds on *Identities: A short story collection*, to imagine and portray ways in which a variety of global African characters—multicultural and multiracial, negotiate their sense of self and belonging. They do so within a world where their sense of rootedness and belonging must cross racial, cultural, continental and generational divides. My hope is to share some narratives of the possibilities that emerge from this creative space I have experienced and exist in. I hope to portray global Africans in more shades of the bridge-building, resilient capacity, ingenuity and love we bring to a world that desperately needs these qualities. This short story collection also highlights the agency and choices global Africans must regularly make to transcend artificial boundaries and claim belonging in our world.

BOOKS BY DR YABOME GILPIN-JACKSON

Identities: A Short Story Collection

Identities is a short story collection of global African experiences.

The stories in this collection evoke the lived experiences of Africans of diverse backgrounds, races, ethnicities and identities.
It explores everyday identity concerns of diasporan Africans such as experiences of being asked: Where are you from? immigrant and refugee integration, personal vs. ascribed social standing, remittance responsibilities, traditional vs. contemporary cultural values and many others.

This collection is ultimately about the experiences of bridging, balancing and weaving together the multiple strands that form contemporary African identities on and off the continent. Identities features a companion guide, ideal for educators and book club enthusiasts or even an individual reader—to delve deeper into the themes that Identities provokes.

Book and guide available on Amazon.

We Will Lead Africa Book Series

Dr Yabome Gilpin-Jackson is the Initiator, Co-Founder and Lead Editor of We Will Lead Africa.

We Will Lead Africa is a global network and social enterprise, founded by the co-editors of the first collection, Yabome Gilpin-Jackson, Sarah Owusu and Judith Okonkwo.

It was established with the intent of curating and sharing stories, and creating networks of everyday African leaders, anywhere in the world, doing work impacting the progress of continental Africa.

Our Vision: *Africans owning and leading our narratives*
Our mission: *Creating platforms for sharing and inspiring everyday African leadership through storytelling*

The We Will Lead Africa team have launched 2 volumes of leaders working for progress of the continent. Their first volume features the stories of 30 everyday African leaders and their second volume captures 32 inspirational stories of 36 everyday African women leaders. A call for submissions for a third volume is already underway.